Valegro

The Little Horse with the Big Dream

The Blueberry Stories: Book One

Carl Hester MBE with Janet Rising

with illustrations by Helena Öhmark

Matador
9 Priory Business Park,
Wistow Road, Kibworth Beauchamp,
Leicestershire. LE8 0RX
Tel: 0116 279 2299
Email: books@troubador.co.uk
Web: www.troubador.co.uk/matador
Twitter: @matadorbooks

ISBN 978 1785898 532

British Library Cataloguing in Publication Data.
A catalogue record for this book is available from the British Library.

Printed and bound in the UK by TJ International, Padstow, Cornwall
Typeset in 12pt Book Antiqua by Troubador Publishing Ltd, Leicester, UK

Matador is an imprint of Troubador Publishing Ltd

This book is dedicated to Dexter, who patiently watched and listened to so many of Blueberry's training sessions

Chapter One

As the horsebox turned off the road the little brown horse, sensing they were slowing down, woke from his doze. Stretching his neck and turning his head sideways he could just see out of the high window. Although it was getting dark and he was still sleepy he could make out high gates opening silently to allow the horsebox along the tree-flanked drive where a further pair of gates stood open in welcome. As the horsebox rumbled on the little horse strained to look out again. He wasn't sure whether he was awake now or still asleep. He caught sight of a horse standing proudly, foreleg lifted high in dance, a glittering, shining horse, changing colour from red to green to blue…

"Where are we?" asked the other horse, a chestnut with a white blaze and two white socks above his front hooves. Before the little horse could answer the horsebox came to a gentle halt; the engine shuddering to silence, and the ramp was lowered, signalling the end of the horses' long journey. As the chestnut was led down the ramp and on to the yard, the little horse listened intently (his ears swivelling like radar) as he was anxious to learn more about his new home. He heard the patter of dog paws, the soothing sounds of human voices reassuring and welcoming the horses and he felt himself relax. He hadn't realised how tense he had been. When his journey had begun early that morning, a long way away in Holland, he hadn't a clue where he might be headed, but this place seemed calm and welcoming. It was, he sensed, a good place.

A girl with freckles and red hair tied back in a pony tail walked up the ramp of the horsebox towards the little brown horse.

"Come on then," she said, patting him on

2

the neck and untying his rope, "you don't want to spend the night in here, do you? We've got a nice stable ready for you," and she led the little horse down the ramp to the neat rectangular yard where horses looked intently over their half doors, determined not to miss the latest batch of recruits.

"I wish they'd stop staring!" said the chestnut horse with the blaze and two white socks. He had always been quite shy. He lowered his head in an attempt to make himself appear smaller – which was tricky as even at two years old, the chestnut stood over 16.2 hands high or 1.65cm at the wither. The little brown horse, by contrast, wished he were taller. He'd always been the smallest of all the colts at the farm in Holland, and he couldn't wait to grow and catch them up. He had overheard people remarking on his lack of height, and comparing him to the other horses. Why was being tall such a good thing? He had no idea, but it seemed to matter. Even though the horses in the stables all stared at him, and there were lots of people he didn't recognise in the yard, the little brown horse lifted his head and drew himself up proudly.

"Lydia, it's the corner stable for the little one," someone said, and the girl led the little brown horse into a lit stable, checking him all over to make sure he hadn't suffered any injuries on

3

his long trip. Taking off the travelling boots the horse wore to protect him, she noticed he had a tiny white sock on his near (left) foreleg, a longer sock on his off (right) foreleg and two high socks – almost stockings, not quite reaching his hocks, on both hind legs. On his face was a white star which ran into a long strip down the very centre of his face, ending in a white splodge towards his left nostril. There was also an unusual white patch under his tummy, which you could only see when he was upside down and rolling in the field or in his stable.

The little horse was relieved to see a full net of hay, an automatic drinking container and a deep bed of wood shavings, banked up around the walls for comfort. He'd been right; this was a good place! Looking out over his stable door, he watched as the people settled all the other horses for the night. Rugs were straightened, shavings swept up, bolts checked, buckets gathered and put away with purpose. A variety of dogs shadowed the people and a cat sauntered across the yard as though it owned the place – until one of the dogs, large and fierce-looking, gave chase. The cat merely leapt up onto a vacant stable door and flicked its tail at the dog which stopped and turned around, pretending it hadn't actually been chasing its tail after all. Gradually, the lights were all turned off and the people drifted away, but Lydia came back to wish him goodnight.

"You're a compact package, all right," said Lydia, leaning on the half-door. "I can't wait to see what Carl has to say about you when he gets back tomorrow."

The little brown horse ate half his hay and drank some water. Hearing the sounds of the other horses in the yard moving around in their stables and chewing their hay made him feel safe and secure. Then, realising how tired he was after his journey, he lay down on the deep bed of shavings and drifted off into a deep sleep, dreaming about a glittering horse which changed colour as it danced.

Chapter Two

People with hens and cockerels never need an alarm clock – and at Brook Mill Stables the cockerels took their job seriously. The little brown horse awoke with a start as daybreak was heralded with a series of *cock-a-doodle-dos*, and he struggled to his feet in alarm, wondering where he was. Then he remembered his long journey and arrival the night before. Looking out over his stable door, he noticed that no-one else seemed concerned about the noise – apart from his chestnut friend with the blaze and two white socks. His eyes were wide and he could hear him snort, even though he was right on the other side of the stable yard.

'Get a grip!' the little brown horse muttered, and he gave himself a shake which started at his nose, trembled through his ears and neck, along the length of his body and finished with a flick of his tail. Pale shavings flew off his mane and tail and floated down around him like snowflakes, but some still stubbornly clung to his coat. Soon, people arrived on the yard and breakfast was served. The horses whinnied and stamped, urging the grooms to hurry, but as one of the new inhabitants the little brown horse didn't think it would be good manners to be impatient. He was thrilled to receive a bucket of feed, and he chomped his way through the chaff and nuts and mix. This really was a good place!

Mucking out is an important part of any stable routine, and at Brook Mill was carried out smartly and quickly. The little brown horse soon had a lovely clean bed of shavings, and swift brooms in expert hands had the yard immaculate once more. Then the yard was deserted and quiet descended as all the humans hurried to eat their own breakfasts.

With breakfast over, the humans came once more onto the yard and the little brown horse pricked up his ears at the sound of a new voice. No, he corrected himself; this was a voice he'd heard before. Stretching his neck over the door, the little horse could see a tall man talking to

Lydia, the fierce-looking dog leaning against his long legs. He'd been right, the voice belonged to the man who had come to see him in Holland, who had said nice things to him and patted his neck. His voice had held the little horse's attention. He had no idea he would ever see this man again – yet here he was! It appeared that this time, the little brown horse had come to see him.

The chestnut horse with the white blaze and two white socks was led out of his stable and through the arch of the yard. Then Lydia appeared with a headcollar, and she and the little horse followed the chestnut's footsteps. They passed under the arch and the little brown horse's eyes opened wide as he saw a huge building with a high roof and one open side, and next to this, with a walkway between the two, a large, flat, rectangular arena, surrounded by low hedges. Instead of dirt or grass, the arena was covered with a surface which, when the little horse was led onto it, felt springy and soft underfoot, and his hooves made no sound at all.

The man with the voice he recognised from Holland was there with some other people, and the chestnut horse was being trotted up and down before them. No, the little brown horse corrected himself, there were *two* identical chestnut horses being trotted up and down. It was amazing – as though they were trotting in unison, their steps

8

matching, stride-for-stride. The people watched the chestnut horses with interest. The little brown horse watched all the people.

"Lovely fluent paces, Carl," remarked one of the women. The man who had seen the little horse in Holland nodded.

Carl, thought the little horse. Yes, he remembered now. And then the little brown horse noticed another brown horse in front of him. A little brown horse with a stripe on his face and three – no four – white socks. He wondered who it was.

"Just stand him up for a moment," said Carl, and the groom asked the chestnut horse to stand still, his feet planted as though at each corner of a square, which is the balanced way for a horse to stand. The second chestnut horse did exactly the same. The little horse watched, and decided he could stand like that if he were asked.

"He'll grow a bit more, but he's already well up to height," Carl said, running his hands over the chestnut horse's legs and then standing back to rub his own chin. As he did so the little brown horse noticed another person, who looked exactly like Carl, do the very same thing to the other chestnut horse. Something, the little brown horse told himself, was not quite as it seemed – unless Carl had a twin! The other brown horse – who was quite small, he noticed – stood watching, just as he did.

Suddenly, two dogs ran into the arena, playing and pretending to fight with each other. The two chestnut horses leapt into the air and bucked in unison, almost pulling away from the grooms on the other end of the rope. The little horse felt his own neck tighten and his legs quiver as he watched the dogs, but he didn't move. The dogs were only playing. And then he noticed there were *four* dogs.

"It's all right, he'll get used to them, that's why we have all these distractions around the place," said Carl, kindly. "Everyone needs to expect the unexpected here. This little fellow doesn't mind, do you?" he added, turning to the little horse. "Let's see his paces, Lydia."

The little horse was walked up and down, and then asked to trot. The other brown horse was doing the same thing next to him and the little brown horse realised that somehow, it wasn't another horse. Somehow, he thought, he was seeing himself – because there seemed to be two Lydia's, and that, he thought, wasn't right. The little brown horse trotting next to him, he realised, was himself! Somehow, the long, shiny wall next to the long side of the arena was duplicating everything he saw. It was strange, but it didn't worry him at all. Feeling it was important, the little horse trotted as well as he could, arching his neck while holding his head high, lifting his legs and covering the ground well. When he got back to stand in front of Carl, he arranged his legs in a square without being asked, and listened intently for his opinion. He hoped Carl would say nice things about him, just as he had about the chestnut horse.

"He moves well," said Carl, appreciatively. The little horse puffed his chest out in pride.

"He's very small," said one of the women, shaking her head, "and rather cobby – not terribly refined. He doesn't look much like the stamp of horse to excel in the arena, Carl. Whatever were you thinking, choosing this one?" The little horse felt his heart contract. Glancing in the strange reflecting thing, he realised that he was even smaller than he had imagined. Much smaller than the chestnut horse. What did the woman mean about him being cobby and not refined? Was that good – or bad? He couldn't do anything about it if he didn't understand what it was.

"Yes," agreed Carl, "he does need to grow." He could feel the beginnings of a frown on his forehead. That the little brown horse was smaller, and perhaps more thickset than the others, hadn't escaped his notice when he had seen him in Holland, but he had bought him anyway. There was something about

11

this horse, but Carl couldn't begin to explain what it was. He had seen hundreds – maybe thousands – of horses, and sometimes he got a feeling about one, a feeling that told him that one was special. He'd had the feeling when he'd first seen this little horse but now, a few months later, the horse hadn't grown as much as he had hoped. Carl was tall, he needed a horse which could carry him without making him look as though he was riding a pony.

The little brown horse's heart tightened and he lifted his head to appear taller as Carl continued to look at him without speaking.

"But after all," Carl added, as much to himself as anyone else, "he's only two – there's plenty of time for him to blossom." He said it with conviction, but he still had his doubts. He hoped he hadn't made a mistake buying this one. He had liked him, he still did, but there was no escaping the fact that the horse might not make the height he wanted, even allowing for his young age.

"Nice head, though," said one of the women. "It looks like a seahorse."

There were murmurs of agreement. The tightness in the little horse's heart loosened.

"He seems intelligent, and he does move well," said Carl, "but you need to grow," he added, giving the little horse a pat. A cold shiver ran through the little horse's heart. He didn't know why it mattered so much that Carl should like him, but he sensed that it was important.

"Okay, now for the fun part," announced Carl, putting aside his worries about the brown horse's height for now. He would come to a decision later but now everyone was looking forward to naming the new horses. They already had their posh, breeder's name – the little brown horse had been named Valegro – and this was registered for life, but often these names were long and impossible to use every day. Each horse, on its arrival at Brook Mill Stables, was given a stable name by which it was always known. Last year all newcomers were named after flowers, this year the theme was fruit and vegetables. There was already a Radish, a Plum and an Apple.

"Any suggestions?" asked Carl.

"The chestnut could only be Orange," said one of the grooms.

"Yes," agreed Carl, "he is bright."

"The little one's a funny colour," said someone else.

"I think it's a nice colour," said Carl. "Brown with a blueish tinge."

"He's quite chunky," someone piped up. "How about Pineapple?"

The little brown horse's ears wiggled. Some people, he thought, could be quite rude.

"Definitely *not* Pineapple," said Carl, firmly.

"There aren't any blue fruits or vegetables," said someone else.

"Beetroot's sort of blue," said Lydia.

"How about blackberries?" suggested a groom. "They're blue-ish."

"He's not quite a blackberry, more a *blue*berry," mused Carl, thinking about the ones he had for breakfast each morning. "Yes, I think our little friend is a Blueberry!"

There were nods of agreement all round.

"They're only really one of the gang once they've got names," said Carl. "Orange and Blueberry it is."

The little brown horse liked his new name. Maybe getting a name would mean good luck. It was difficult to have doubts about someone when you've given them a name and now he was called Blueberry he was, Carl had said, one of the gang.

"There you go, Blueberry," said Lydia, leading the little horse back to the stable and giving his neck a pat. "Welcome to the family!"

14

Chapter Three

The next day, Blueberry and Orange were turned out in a paddock to graze and stretch their legs. Orange insisted on walking around the perimeter of the paddock to check there were no hidden monsters or demons to worry about. Newly named Blueberry, deciding to save his energy, stood in the middle and watched his friend make like a sentry. Eventually, Orange stopped hugging the fencing like he was attached to it and declared that they were, for now anyway, safe.

And then he changed his mind. From a hole in the hedge came a procession of one, two, three – a total of seven – strange birds, all legs and neck, grey mottled feathers fluttering in the breeze as they bobbed along the hedge in a line. They weren't hens, Blueberry knew that. These were a similar shape, but whereas the hens were a mixture of colours – some white, others brown or black – these birds were all identical. They looked, the little brown horse thought, as though someone had designed one, and then got fed up with the effort of it all and decided that one design would do.

"What on earth…?" whispered Orange, trembling in fear.

"I don't think you need to worry," said Blueberry, stretching his neck forward to see the strange creatures better, "they look more scared of us than we are of them."

Sure enough, the strange group bobbed their way cautiously across the field in fits and starts and Blueberry could hear them all muttering words of fear and trepidation: "Be careful there… watch your step… did anyone else hear that noise? Mind that, that, that, er shadow thing there… ahhhh… whatever is that… oh no, it's okay, false alarm! I thought we'd had it then… keep up, don't get left behind…" Blueberry couldn't help thinking they reminded him a little of Orange, and he felt sorry that they were so nervous all the time. That just had to be exhausting, he thought.

Their progress of fits and starts changed suddenly to terrified leaps and bounds in all directions as the birds began squawking loudly,

16

their wings flapping as the big, ferocious-looking dog that Blueberry had seen before burst through the hedge towards them, barking in excitement.

"Willow!" boomed a voice. Blueberry turned to see Carl looking over the hedge, and hearing his master's angry tone the dog stopped in its tracks and glanced back in confusion. That he was torn between chasing the birds and obeying his master was obvious.

"I've told you before about chasing the guinea fowl!" roared Carl, and the big dog, Willow, reluctantly turned, his long tail down, taking one last wistful look towards the birds before skulking back to Carl.

Guinea fowl, thought Blueberry. Never seen those before. Can't see them now, he thought, as the guinea fowl had all fluttered into the hedgerow in alarm before Willow could change his mind about obeying Carl. Blueberry heard Orange let out the breath he'd been holding and the big chestnut horse put his head down to graze, the excitement over.

The paddock was right next to the outdoor arena, separated by a hedge, so the two horses could hear sounds from the yard and the arena. For the first hour, however, they both put their heads down to tear at the sweet grass and enjoyed feeling the sun on their backs. Going

17

out in the field is a horse's downtime, and eating grass is one of their favourite things to do. Living in a stable all the time is not natural to horses. Not only do they love the grass, but they enjoy being with their friends and can catch up socially – grooming each other with their teeth to get rid of any itchiness, stretching their legs, playing and making friends. All the horses at Brook Mill enjoyed lots of time in the fields surrounding the stables, allowing them to chill-out and relax which, in turn, helped them to enjoy their work even more. Just like people, horses enjoy a good life-work balance!

After an hour or so tearing at the grass, Blueberry lifted his head to look around and listened to sounds coming from the other side of the hedge. Wandering over, he looked over the top and was totally unprepared for what he saw.

In the arena was a big black horse, and on its back was Carl. Blueberry had seen horses being ridden before, and he looked forward to the day when he would be a grown-up horse and carry a rider. He noticed this horse didn't move in the same way he had ever seen a ridden horse move, or even how a horse trots and canters in the field; head low, legs loose. This horse was moving as though his skeleton was a horizontal spring, tightly coiled so that his hind legs could

18

get closer to his front legs, propelling himself along with controlled energy. The horse's back was high, his head held proudly, neck arched, nose tucked into his chest. The horse moved as though his hooves housed more springs, and his steps were high and light and beautiful to watch – and even though he looked as though he was trotting, he wasn't getting anywhere. He stayed in the same spot, his legs lifting higher and higher. This black horse, under Carl, looked like – Blueberry searched in his brain for the right word – it looked to him as though the horse and Carl were *dancing*. Where had Blueberry seen a dancing horse like the one in the arena? He couldn't quite remember.

"Good boy," Carl whispered, patting the black horse and loosening the reins so the horse could relax. Immediately, the horse became just an ordinary horse again, walking with its head down, stretching its neck.

Blueberry stood and stared. He had played in the fields in Holland with the other colts, he had reared and bucked and pranced with his tail held high like a flag. He had bounced on his legs as though his hooves were made from springs, tucking his chin in to his chest and spinning around on his hind legs at the sheer joy of being a colt and alive and free with his friends. The black horse had performed some of the same movements – but with Carl on his back. And the movements were so beautiful, and so graceful and so... Blueberry was lost for words and his ears dropped either side of his forelock as his brain worked overtime. This horse was an ordinary horse, like he was, yet he transformed into a very different horse when asked by Carl. Could any horse dance like the black horse danced?

Grass was forgotten as Blueberry spent the next half-an-hour watching the horse in the arena and listening to Carl as he talked to his mount. Wandering over, Orange asked him what he found so fascinating, but Blueberry couldn't explain how watching the horse made him feel, and he was afraid that Orange wouldn't understand anyway and might even laugh at him. But Orange surprised him. He too watched Carl and the black horse dancing on the other side of the hedge, and Blueberry could sense that, like he, the chestnut horse was mesmerised by, and amazed at what they were watching.

"Wow," breathed Orange, "do you think we could ever dance like that horse?"

"Maybe," said Blueberry. But as soon as he said it, he knew he would only be able to do that if Carl were to help him, if Carl were to teach him. Losing interest, Orange wandered off again

20

to eat more grass, but Blueberry kept watching. As he did so, he realised that his own hooves were tingling and he felt himself mirroring the horse in the arena, lifting his own legs as the black horse lifted his. "One foreleg together with the opposite hind leg," Blueberry muttered to himself as his legs quivered and lifted slightly, "then swap to the other two legs... this is hard, but that horse makes it look easy!"

Suddenly, Blueberry became aware that he was being watched. Turning his head he saw a small dog, the colour of Carl's long, tan boots, looking at him from the gate. Blueberry's hooves stopped and he felt a bit silly, especially as the little dog was winking at him. Was he making fun of him? Perhaps his efforts to copy the amazing black horse *were* a bit of a joke. Before he could say anything, the dog turned around and disappeared back under the gate towards the yard.

I don't care if I look silly, Blueberry decided, and he was going to return to his attempts at dancing, only Carl and the black horse had left the arena so he had to rely on his memory to guide him.

Chapter Four

When Lydia came to catch him and bring him into the stable, Blueberry realised he was still hungry. He hadn't eaten as much grass as Orange. Luckily, there was a small feed waiting for him in his clean stable, and a net of hay to munch. After a doze and a drink, Blueberry stuck his head over his stable door to watch the other horses being tacked up in their saddles and bridles, then leaving the yard to be ridden – and realised they would probably move under their riders like the black horse had moved under Carl. He wished he could go and see them. He wished he could *be* them. He especially wished he was as tall as they were.

They returned after a while, and from his stable in the corner of the yard Blueberry watched them being washed down in the special area between the arena and the stables, then standing under glowing red lights which warmed and dried them. Glowing red lights... there was a glowing red horse in Blueberry's memory... he just couldn't remember where and when he had seen it.

Suddenly, Blueberry was aware of the small dog, the same one who had watched him from the paddock gate, sitting in the yard, leaning against the wall. Tan in colour, short of leg, the dog was looking at him again. And yes, Blueberry saw, taking another look, the dog was still *winking* at him. The little horse glanced around – he didn't want to make a fool of himself. Maybe the dog was looking and winking at someone else. But no, there was no-one else there; the dog was definitely winking at him. Why? There was only one way to find out...

"Hello," said Blueberry.

"Uh-ummm," replied the dog, still winking.

"Can I help you?" Blueberry asked, politely.

"How, exactly?" replied the dog.

This stumped Blueberry. He hadn't really meant that he wanted to help the dog; it was just good manners to ask. "Er, well... um..." Blueberry tailed off, not knowing how to answer.

"You're not very big for a dressage horse," said the dog. Blueberry thought this odd on two counts: one, the dog wasn't exactly leggy itself, so that was quite rude, and two, he didn't know what a dressage horse was, and so certainly wasn't sure he was actually one. Perhaps the dog had mistaken him for someone else. He thought he might just stick his head back into his stable and go back to eating hay and dismiss the dog as a bit bonkers – but then he changed his mind. Maybe, he thought, he could learn something. The second option was the more intelligent one, he decided. He'd be doubly stupid if he let the opportunity pass him by. He took a deep breath and risked it.

"What's a dressage horse?" he asked.

The dog made a sound between a snort and a laugh. "Oh dear," she said, sighing and shaking her head. "Oh dear, oh dear, oh dear…" and she stood up and came closer, looking up at Blueberry so that he could see the mistake he had made. The dog hadn't been winking at him at all. The poor thing had only one eye – not that this seemed to bother her. Where the missing eye used to be could be seen a criss-cross of old-looking stitches. It seemed the dog had lost the eye some time ago. Blueberry was thankful he hadn't made any reference to the dog winking – how embarrassing would that have been? He didn't think it polite to ask about the missing eye. Best, he thought, just to ignore it altogether.

"A dressage horse, my diminutive friend, is what you saw in the arena this morning, the horse whose skilled and practised movements you attempted to copy," said the dog. "A dressage horse," she continued, standing shakily on three legs in order to wave a front paw around the yard to indicate all the horses in it, "is what we have here. *This* is a dressage yard. *These* are dressage horses. *You* are here to train to be a dressage horse. That, if you stay, is your *job*."

Blueberry felt his muzzle tighten and his chin wiggle as his brain got to work. He always did this whenever he was thinking. The more his muzzle tightened, and the more his chin wiggled, the more his brain was whirling, and right now, his brain was in overdrive. It was whirling so much, it almost hurt.

"So *dressage* is what you call all those amazing movements the horses make under their riders?" asked Blueberry, risking more canine ridicule just to make sure.

"Got it!" said the dog. "At last," she added, rolling her remaining eye.

"So I'm going to learn all those dance moves," said Blueberry, as much to himself as anyone else. "Wow!" There was a feeling

25

in his heart he had never experienced before. Blueberry felt a flutter, then a glow. It spread from his heart, through his legs right down to his feet and he wanted to lift them up and dance right there. He, Blueberry, was destined to be a *dressage* horse. How amazing was that? It was, the dog had said, his *job*. He felt like he might burst! Then he remembered what else the dog had said.

"What do you mean," Blueberry asked, half wondering if he really wanted to know the answer, "*if I stay?*"

"If Carl thinks you've got what it takes," said the dog, casually lifting a hind leg and scratching behind one ear.

Blueberry's heart fluttered again, but in a different way. He felt a bit short of breath. "You mean, I might *not* be able to dance?" he asked, scared of the answer.

The dog nodded. "It seems harsh kiddo," she said, "but not everyone who comes here makes the big time. It's tough in the dressage world and there's only room for the best. Of course, it's not the end of the world if you don't make it here, someone else will want you and you'll still be able to do dressage, but not at the highest level. Carl has room only for the best and, as a top Olympic rider, he needs horses which want success as much as he does. Plus,

26

you're not exactly the tallest equine I've ever seen, hardly more than a pony at the moment and Carl's worried about that. So my question to you, kiddo, is dressage really what you want to do?"

Before Blueberry could answer the little dog got up and started across the yard. It appeared the lesson was over, and Blueberry didn't feel it was the right time to ask her to explain what an Olympic rider was.

"What's your name?" Blueberry called after her.

"Lulu," the dog replied as she disappeared into the feed room to search out dropped and tasty nuggets of horse feed between the feed bins, leaving Blueberry to his see-saw of emotions as he swung between the high of imagining himself dancing like he had seen the black horse dance, and the low of remembering the words which had followed him from Holland: *Yes*, Carl had said, *he does need to grow*.

Chapter Five

Blueberry woke up in the middle of the night. Something was wrong. He waited until his eyes got used to the dark and he could make out his stable walls. There were no sounds. Everything was quiet. There was nothing wrong with his stable, or in the yard. Whatever was wrong was wrong with him. His legs felt wobbly, his head hurt and he felt cold – then hot – then cold again. Sinking to his knees Blueberry lay in his stable and shivered, waiting for morning to come and for Lydia to find and help him. But when the cockerels announced the daybreak, it wasn't Lydia who found him.

Well before the humans were due on the yard, Blueberry could hear the sound of scratching at his stable door, and a whining sound alerting Carl, who had got up early to walk the dogs, to look into the little horse's stable.

"What is it Lulu?" Blueberry heard Carl ask – and the moment he caught sight of Blueberry lying down, his muzzle resting on his bed, his breathing laboured and his eyes half-closed, Carl was in the stable and on his mobile phone, urging the vet to visit as soon as possible.

Soon, everyone knew Blueberry was ill, and everyone was worried. The little horse looked so sad and poorly and his friend Orange called over from his stable on the other side of the yard, telling him he was thinking of him. Poor Blueberry was too ill to reply. His head hurt, his whole body ached, he just wanted to lie down and be left alone. But nobody did. Everyone cared for him too much.

"Don't worry, kiddo," Blueberry heard Lulu call, "the vet's on her way. She'll get you up and dancing in no time." But even the thought of dancing had no effect on Blueberry, who just closed his eyes and groaned.

"It's probably an infection," said the vet, after examining Blueberry and taking his temperature, which was high. "I'll give the little chap an injection and I'll take a blood sample back to the lab. Keep him warm, keep him quiet. I'll let you know the results of the blood test as soon as I can. I'd better check the other one which travelled with him while I'm here," she added, "just to be sure he's okay."

Orange demonstrated how okay he was by rearing up on his hind legs as soon as the vet approached him. He had a bit of a phobia about vets.

"Good job the poorly chap isn't like this one," the vet said, gritting her teeth and trying for the third time to take Orange's temperature. Eventually, he was declared fit – for now – but the grooms were instructed to keep a strict eye on him.

Blueberry lay on his bed and dozed. The injection didn't make him feel any better, just sleepy, and he drifted off to sleep between hearing the other horses come and go, to and from the yard for their exercise and work. Lydia came in to check on him several times a day, and all the other grooms looked in whenever they passed his stable, but for the next few days nothing much changed. Blueberry was very ill indeed.

The vet came and gave him more injections, Carl looked anxiously over the half door and told him to hang on in there, and Lydia sat in the corner of the stable and spoke softly to him, so he knew everyone cared. Lulu also found

30

a way into his stable from the back – she had made Lulu-sized entrances around the whole yard so she could keep an eye on things – and she sat with him when Lydia was busy working. Blueberry could feel the dog's cold nose on his neck, and was touched. Clearly, the little dog's gruff manner hid a softer side.

"I took you for a fighter, little horse," Lulu whispered to him, "don't let me down. A dressage horse needs to be tough. You can make it if you have the right attitude – you have to fight for what you want. Come on, Blueberry," she added, when the little horse's breathing got worse. "Everyone wants you to get better. Come on!"

Hearing Lulu say these things made a huge difference to Blueberry. Instead of keeping his eyes closed and drifting into sleep, he opened them and thought about being a dressage horse. Instead of lying down feeling sorry for himself, after a few days he struggled to his feet, determined to show everyone that, although he might not be tall, he was strong and he had a fighting spirit. He walked over to his half door and made an effort to look out, to watch what was going on and when Carl came down to the yard in the morning, the little horse managed a whispered whinny of hello.

"Up at last, you lazy fellow," said Carl kindly,

fondling the little horse's ears. He was relieved to see Blueberry up on his feet – it seemed he was on the way to getting better.

Chapter Six

Lydia was thrilled to see that Blueberry was on the road to recovery, and everyone else on the yard came by to wish him well – but he was far from being back to his old self. For the next two weeks, Lydia nursed Blueberry and, as he got stronger, he got cheekier. Being the centre of attention encouraged the little horse to take liberties and he nudged Lydia when she came in to check on him, and pulled the sleeve of her jumper with his teeth.

"Hey, stop that!" cried Lydia. But she couldn't

be cross with her patient for long. She was just happy he felt well enough to be cheeky. It was a sure sign that the little horse was on the mend, and everyone breathed a huge, collective, sigh of relief.

"Come on," said Lydia, leading Blueberry out on his headcollar and long lead rein, "some Dr Green will be good for you."

Blueberry didn't know who Dr Green was, but he wasn't looking forward to another vet looking him over. The vet who visited him regularly was okay, but she had a nasty habit of sticking needles into him without asking first. But instead of seeing another vet, Lydia led Blueberry down the drive to graze on some long grass. Because grass is so good for horses, it is known as Dr Green!

Blueberry tore at the grass. It tasted so good and he could almost feel it working some magic as he swallowed it. Lydia wandered along beside him as the little horse munched his way along the verge to the drive. He hadn't been this side of the yard since his arrival in the horsebox. The stable yard was behind him, Carl's house in front of him, and the driveway led off into the distance. Suddenly, Blueberry could see another horse. Looking up, he was puzzled. It was a horse – at least it looked like a horse – and yet it didn't move. And it glinted in the sunlight like no other horse Blueberry had ever seen. Moving closer, Blueberry could see that the horse wasn't real, but made from a shiny metal which glistened and sparkled as it reflected the sun's rays. It stood proud, one foreleg raised, his head high. And it looked familiar…

Suddenly, Blueberry realised he was looking at the horse in his dream, the dancing horse – only this one was silver. The one in his dream had been red… then green… then… And then Blueberry realised he hadn't dreamt about the horse at all; he had seen it for real, the night he had arrived at Brook Mill Stables. This was the horse which had shone in different colours. Blueberry stretched out his nose and sniffed the silver horse's nose. It smelt of nothing at all.

"Most horses are a bit nervous of The Silver Dancer when they first meet him," said Lydia, "but you're not, are you Blueberry? You really are a clever little horse. Now come on, you're supposed to be eating grass!"

Blueberry loved getting praise from Lydia – but he would have loved it even more if only she'd managed not to describe him as *little* when she spoke to him!

When he went back to his stable Blueberry felt much better. The grass had acted like a tonic. It had been good to stretch his legs – and he couldn't stop thinking about the metallic horse.

When Lulu passed his stable on her way to the field to enjoy her daily sniff-a-thon, Blueberry asked her about his new discovery.

"The Silver Dancer?" said Lulu, sitting down and scratching behind one ear with a hind leg. "You've met The Silver Dancer, have you?"

"What can you tell me about him?" asked Blueberry.

"He's art," explained Lulu, managing not to explain at all. When she saw Blueberry's confused expression, and noticed his chin wobbling (Lulu had already clocked that a wobbling chin on Blueberry reflected intense thinking), Lulu sighed and put her field trip on hold. "Art," she explained, "is what some humans like to do – make stuff from other stuff to look like real stuff. Only it isn't."

"What's it for?" asked Blueberry.

"Looking at. Admiring. Showing other people. It's not actually *for* anything. It's a *concept*," Lulu said. Blueberry decided that the more questions he asked, the less he seemed to learn. They just prompted more questions.

"Some clever person made The Silver Dancer, created to p*iaffe* forever," Lulu continued, "and when people come here, they all want one. Humans are like that. One gets something and then everyone wants one. If something is unique – and that means there's

36

only one of them – " Lulu added, noticing Blueberry's quizzical chin, "the more valuable it becomes. If everyone could make a horse like The Silver Dancer, then probably no-one would want one, and copies aren't as valuable as the first, the original. It's the same with dressage horses. No-one is impressed by a horse that just walks and trots like any other horse. But they are impressed by a horse which can do all the moves better than the others, one which gets the best possible scores in competitions. They're all chasing that. But not everyone can train one. Carl can. He can train horses like the clever person can make art like The Silver Dancer. And the horses Carl trains go on to be the best. They're originals; not copies. Carl's an artist too; he just works with real horses, not wire and silver metal."

"But I don't think Carl will train me," said Blueberry. "I need to be bigger if I want to be a dressage horse, everyone says I'm small."

"*Compact*," corrected Lulu, sternly.

"And chunky," added Blueberry.

"With great chunkiness comes great power," Lulu told him, solemnly. "And vice versa, of course."

Blueberry blinked several times. "What does that mean?"

"It's Latin," explained Lulu, without explaining

37

at all. Blueberry made a decision not to go there.

"Look," said Lulu, staring at Blueberry with her one eye, "don't let anyone tell you what you are, or define you – only *you* know what you want to be. If you want to be a top dressage horse you will – but you won't if you doubt yourself. You want it? Go do it! If you're not like the other dressage horses, so what? Break the mould! You know what Carl says? *Make it happen.* He says some people *want* it to happen, some *wish* it would happen and others *make* it happen. Which are you? Just wishing – or even worse, doubting – isn't going to get you far. Deciding what you want is the first step – and it sounds like you've already decided. The second thing is to come up with a plan to get it – and then work hard to make that plan work. So what if you're small? Only Blueberry can be Blueberry – be a one-off, like The Silver Dancer. Be an original, not a copy!"

Blueberry's chin almost turned inside out. He decided he'd think very carefully about what Lulu had said later that night, when the yard was quiet and everyone was asleep. It was important, he knew that much. There seemed a lot to it, though.

"One more thing…" said Blueberry, just as Lulu had got up and was looking once more at the fields where intoxicating smells beckoned,

"… was The Silver Dancer ever, um, red, or green or something?" It sounded stupid when he said it. Surely then he'd be called the red or green dancer.

"Technology," said Lulu, making her way through the arch, her nose twitching. "Lights," she added over her shoulder, and once again Blueberry had no idea what she meant. And it was only when Lulu's tail vanished from sight that he wished he asked her what *piaffe* meant.

Chapter Seven

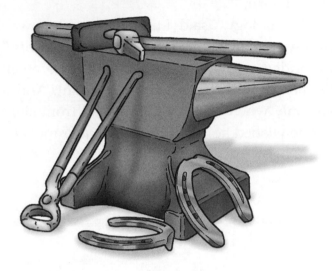

No two days at Brook Mill Stables were ever the same. Blueberry always put his head over his half door on the days the farrier came to visit and watched him work from his van which was crammed with tools, parked in the yard. Horses were led out to have their worn shoes removed and their hooves trimmed before having new shoes fitted. Blueberry was used to having his feet handled – he had learned his lessons in Holland – but he was fascinated to watch the shoeing, closing his nostrils against the smell of the smoke when the farrier measured how the hot shoes fitted against the horses' bare hooves.

"Doesn't that hurt?" he asked Uthopia, a year older than him and getting shoes fitted for the first time.

"You'd think so, wouldn't you?" replied the almost black stallion. "But no, it doesn't. It didn't even hurt when the farrier nailed the shoes on. I do feel a bit strange with them on my hooves, though. They make my legs heavy and I keep forgetting they're on and leaving my hooves behind. I had to lift them a bit higher at first to compensate for the extra weight, but it's getting better now, now I'm getting used to it."

Blueberry couldn't wait to get his first set of shoes. It would mean he was grown up enough to start work – Uthopia had told him he had been sent away to another yard nearby where he had learned to carry a rider, and now he was being trained by Carl. Blueberry was jealous. He couldn't wait to do all the things the older horses did. They all clattered across the yard in their shoes, whereas he just padded across quietly, hardly making a sound. Sometimes, his feet felt a bit sore when he walked on the gravel and concrete. Orange, of course, was also barefoot, but he wasn't keen to get his first shoe fitting.

"Not looking forward to that day," he snorted, when Blueberry mentioned it. Did you see all that horrid smoke? I know Uthopia says it doesn't hurt, but honestly, it must do!"

41

"I don't think it can," argued Blueberry. "Lydia is always saying how important our hooves and feet are, and if our hooves don't work, we don't work."

"Hummmmm, well, we'll know soon enough," Orange said grimly, shaking his head.

The farrier wasn't the only visitor to the yard. The equine physiotherapist – referred to as the physio – was booked for fortnightly appointments, and all the working horses were treated to a massage. When Blueberry asked Lulu what she did, the little dog was happy to explain.

"Lot of muscles under that skin of yours," she began, and Blueberry lowered his head to look at his chest and around at his sides. As he did so, he noticed his skin rippling – or, more accurately – his muscles under the skin.

"See?" said Lulu. "The working horses use those muscles so they need to be in tip-top condition. Muscles help a dressage horse perform all those amazing movements and the more highly trained the dressage horse, the more muscular they are. Muscles are your power, your tools, your energy. No muscles equals no performance. But it's not just about strength – oh no! A dressage horse has to have control over those muscles. Sometimes a muscle strains, or gets a little tight, and this affects a dressage horse's ability to move well. The physio can detect any problems, and she feels for muscular knots and kinks, ironing them out in a massage, or catching any injuries before they can develop into something more serious. Carl leaves nothing to chance here, all the horses are athletes and get treated as such. Everything has to be in top working order to ensure each horse can give its best. Understand?"

Blueberry nodded. There was even more to being a dressage horse than he thought.

"And don't forget the solarium," Lulu added. "It's not just for drying you off after you've been washed down, the heat is good for your muscles, too. But hey, you don't need to worry too much about the physio yet. You won't be seeing her until you're working properly."

Blueberry already knew about the solarium. The warm, red lights had warmed him after Lydia had given him a bath one day, when he'd come in from the field all muddy. Lulu had sneaked up beside him to enjoy their warmth, too. The lights had made him glow – and Blueberry had suddenly realised it was coloured lights that made the amazing Silver Dancer glow in different colours. *Technology*, Lulu had said. Blueberry was quite proud to have worked out for himself what she had meant.

"Don't think horses everywhere get this

43

treatment," Lulu told him, standing on three legs, one back leg scratching behind her ear in an impressive display of controlled balance. (Blueberry couldn't help noticing that Lulu scratched behind her ears a lot. He wondered whether he could get Lydia to give his friend a bit of a groom, to help out.) "Your average horse in the field never sees a solarium or physio, kiddo. You're one of the privileged few."

Blueberry hadn't known what to say about that. He liked being one of the privileged few, but he was sad to think of the other horses which didn't get the benefit of a physio or get to enjoy the amazing solarium. He did like the solarium, it made him feel so warm and well.

There were days when the horsebox was driven onto the gravel outside Carl's house – Blueberry could just see it through the archway if he craned his neck to the left – and the grooms spent a while bouncing between the tack room and the horsebox with saddles, bridles, trunks and boxes. Then, one or two of the horses – dressed in rugs, boots, tail and poll guards – would be loaded, the ramp raised and the horsebox would set out for somewhere Lulu called a *competition*. Sometimes it returned with the horses that same day – occasionally very late in the evening – and at other times it would be gone for days. Blueberry noticed that

44

on its return, someone would always bring a collection of big ribbons in from the horsebox cab and hang them up in the tack room.

"Rosettes," explained Lulu, sighing sometimes at how much she had to tell the little brown horse. There seemed to be no end to his questions, but she realised this meant her friend was intelligent and loved to learn and she didn't want to discourage that. "The red ones are the best – actually, the red, white and blue ones are the *very* best, especially if there's a sash to go with them. It means the horse has won a class, or even a championship. That's what top dressage horses do; they win dressage classes," she said. "It means they're the best of all the horses in the class. It's what all dressage horses want to do, win classes. You get it?"

Blueberry nodded – but it was very difficult to understand about these things when he only went in the stable or the field, and had no idea what it was like at a competition, or any inkling of how a dressage horse won a class. It really was confusing. But Blueberry hoped it would all become clear in the future. When he became Carl's dressage horse he was sure he would learn all these things. It just made it more exciting, and it made him want to learn more and more. He couldn't wait!

Orange could.

"You don't think we'll have to go to competitions, do you?" he whispered to Blueberry one day, as they both watched a horse walking up the ramp into the horsebox. "I mean, I know we want to be able to dance like the other horses, but I'm not sure I want to dance anywhere but here. What if there are lots of people watching? I lose confidence when there are people watching me."

"But you'll know what to do by then," said Blueberry, hoping he was right. "The only horses which go to the competitions are the ones which have been trained. Haven't you noticed?"

"Some are further along in their training than others," said Orange. "Linen is only a couple of years older than us, and he's going to competitions."

"Maybe they have different competitions for different horses, depending on how well they are trained," suggested Blueberry. "That makes sense, doesn't it?"

"Hmmmm, I suppose," said Orange. "I hope you're right."

Blueberry couldn't understand Orange's attitude. He couldn't think of anything more exciting than going to a competition – whatever it was – and showing off his training with Carl. He was sure it would be brilliant! He longed to

46

ask Linen more about the whole concept of going to competitions, but he was usually turned out in the field with Orange, so didn't get a chance.

Chapter Eight

For the next year, Blueberry and Orange enjoyed their time growing up in the stable yard and fields at Brook Mill Stables. Blueberry continued to watch the dressage horses whenever he could. Sometimes he was turned out in a field too far away to see the arena where Carl trained, and sometimes the horses worked in the big indoor arena – but other times he and Orange grazed in the field adjoining the outdoor arena, and Blueberry could watch and be inspired by the horses working. He wasn't the only one who watched. Willow and Lulu were never far away from Carl either. They were usually curled up by his legs if he was teaching, or sitting on the seat at the end of the arena if he was riding. No wonder Lulu knew so much, thought Blueberry. She never missed a lesson.

Most of the time Carl rode the horses himself

but he wasn't the only person who rode the horses, sometimes Carl taught his trainees to ride on his horses. He was very busy and Monday, Tuesday, Thursday and Friday afternoons and all day Wednesday and Saturday he taught other people to ride their own horses that they brought to the yard in a horsebox or trailer. No matter what was going on, the little brown horse watched and learned.

He learned that the riders were always encouraged to work *with* the horses, and although Carl didn't expect the horses to do all the work, they had to do their part. It was the riders' job to sit still, ride as well as they could, in balance, with sympathy, to guide their mounts and to make it easy for them to carry out all the paces and movements they asked for. They would never ask too much, but always encourage their mounts, relaxing and rewarding when the horses had understood something challenging, or when they had done their very best. It was the riders' job to entice the fabulous natural movements from the horses that looked amazing and thrilled Blueberry – but in return the horses had to do their part.

Everyone was expected to give their all and to work hard. This was the only way everyone could discover how good they were – to realise, Carl said, their *true potential*. Blueberry thought very hard about this and realised, from watching the lessons, that the riders and horses achieved better results because of this philosophy. There was no room for anyone at Brook Mill who thought dressage was easy, or for anyone who thought that they were so talented they didn't have to try very hard, or had little to learn. Even Carl said he was learning all the time! And Carl always advised his pupils to listen to their mounts and get feedback through their seat, legs and hands, to learn what their horses were capable of, to discover what they wanted to give and what they found difficult.

Riding was a partnership, Blueberry learnt, and a partnership he couldn't wait to experience. How wonderful it must be, he thought, to work with a rider; to understand what they wanted you to do and be able to give what they asked for especially, he sighed, if that rider was Carl. Blueberry could hardly wait until he was old enough to learn the movements he saw his friends perform.

When he grazed near the arena, Blueberry was often joined by Lulu on one of her sniff-a-thons. Sometimes she was too busy to talk – when the scent of wild things was strong, or she wasn't in the mood to answer questions – but at other times she was happy to explain what the horses were doing.

"There are many different types of trot," Lulu began one day, seeing Blueberry's chin quiver as Carl asked for a collected trot from one rider, and an extended trot from another. "You can see that Mimosa is taking short, controlled steps – that's a collected trot, but Linen there, taking those long strides, is in…"

"… extended trot!" finished Blueberry, rather pleased with himself for understanding at last.

"Well, you obviously don't need my help," sniffed Lulu.

"Oh I do, Lulu, don't be upset. You're a great teacher," soothed Blueberry, anxious not to upset the little dog. "What is Linen doing now?" he added, seeing the grey horse go into yet another version of trot, with extravagant yet hesitant strides, seeming to hover in mid-air for the briefest of seconds at every stride.

"Ahh, well now, that's the *passage*," explained Lulu, nodding her head, pronouncing it pass-*arge* "That, kiddo, is a very advanced movement, very difficult."

Blueberry's chin wobbled again. "But I can do that," he said, trying not to sound too smug. He knew he could do passage, he had done it in the field yesterday when he'd been playing with Orange. And Orange had done it too. Blueberry decided not to let Lulu know that Orange could do it.

"Well of course you can," said Lulu.

That wasn't at all what Blueberry had expected to hear. He had expected Lulu to be impressed or, at the very least, surprised.

"Every horse can do it," Lulu continued. "Every horse can do all the movements you see in the arena, they're all natural. The difficulty comes when you try to do it with a rider on your back. And doing it in *harmony* with a rider on your back. And doing it in harmony with a rider on your back – and *brilliantly*, so brilliantly that you wow the judges' socks off so they give you a higher score than all the other horses. That's the tricky bit!"

"What judges?" asked Blueberry, wondering how he could ever wow their socks off, and why that was important. He had socks, four of them, but he hoped he'd never be so wowed that they'd come right off. What a horrid thought! But Lulu had grown bored and was already half-way across the field, nose down, on the trail of something or someone unknown. It seemed to Blueberry that the more he learned, the less he knew. It was very frustrating – but he was determined to learn everything he could.

It was difficult, this dressage, he thought. But he wouldn't give up, and he would, he decided, be as good at dressage as he possibly could. So he went back to watching the lessons and stored

52

up lots of questions for Lulu to sigh at in future. If Carl said everyone had to give their all, Blueberry decided he would start now, rather than wait until his proper lessons. That way, he told himself, he'd have a head start on the other horses when he was finally in the arena with Carl, and hopefully that would impress him. Could this plan make up for his lack of size? He was disappointed to see that he was still much smaller than Orange, even though he knew he was growing. The trouble was, Orange was growing, too. The little brown horse desperately hoped his plan to distract Carl from his small stature wouldn't let him down.

Chapter Nine

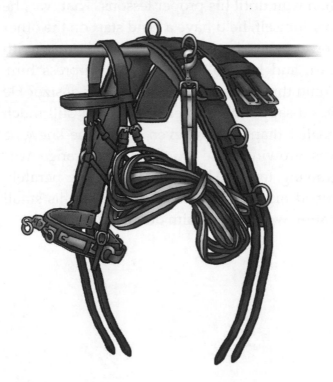

One bright summer day, Lydia led Blueberry out to the yard where the horsebox stood, its ramp down, a deep bed of straw inside. At Lydia's bidding, Blueberry walked up the ramp, wondering what adventure awaited him. When Orange was led up the ramp to stand beside him, they wondered together.

"What's going on?" asked Orange, his head

high, his eyes wide, anxious as always about anything new.

"Stop worrying," said Blueberry, tucking into the haynet, thoughtfully provided. "Lydia's with us and she doesn't seem bothered at all." After a short drive, Lydia lowered the horsebox ramp and came in to untie Orange. She soon returned for Blueberry.

"Now, little Blueberry," whispered Lydia, "you be a good boy with Sandra, and learn all your lessons well so you can come back and begin your higher education."

Blueberry was intrigued. Lessons? Higher education? What was in store for the pair of them?

Just as humans go to different schools throughout their young lives to learn different things, so do horses. In Holland, both Blueberry and Orange had learned lots of lessons about good manners; how to be led, how to lift up their hooves, how to behave correctly and politely around people. They had been handled and taught by knowledgeable people, so they had learned without even realising they were being taught. Now they were three-and-a-half years old it was time for them to further their education – to learn how to carry a rider.

These early lessons are important, for they determine a horse's entire ridden future. If these early lessons are not done well, by an experienced and sympathetic trainer, the horse may never have the right attitude for a good working relationship with any future riders. In fact, he could even learn bad habits which would make his ridden life difficult. With so many horses and riders to train, not to mention a hectic competing schedule, Carl ensured his horses had the best possible start to their training with an experienced trainer of young horses he trusted.

Young horse trainer Sandra not only knew her craft, she also valued each and every horse she trained as individuals, spotting their strengths and encouraging their personalities, while all the time ensuring they learned their lessons in a relaxed and happy environment. Nothing was rushed and the horses all enjoyed their lessons. Blueberry could hardly contain his excitement when her realised he was going to carry a rider for the first time.

Before that, Orange and Blueberry were taught to go on the lunge. That is, they learned how to move well and correctly in a large circle, listening to the trainer standing in the centre at the end of the lunge line, learning the commands to walk, trot, canter and halt. Lungeing, and then progressing to long-reining, helped the horses to strengthen and use their muscles correctly, to move with a steady stride and to listen to their trainer. They were both used to wearing a roller on the lunge and when long-reined so they didn't mind the girth around their middle when they progressed to wearing a saddle, even though it did flap and made more noise – which freaked out Orange enough to promote a bucking fit. Sandra didn't tell him off, knowing he would get used to it. Wearing a saddle, however, made Blueberry feel like a very grown-up horse, and he hoped it wouldn't be too long before Carl would be sitting on his.

And then came the exciting day when Blueberry was actually ridden! With Sandra at his head, her assistant Greg was given a gentle leg-up so he could lean across the little brown horse's back. Blueberry felt his weight – he wasn't very heavy – and looking around he could see his legs dangling down his nearside. Sandra made a fuss of him and told him what a good boy he was, but Blueberry didn't mind at all. He wished Greg would throw his leg over his back and sit up on him properly, so he could show everyone exactly how fine he was with it all. Of course, Sandra didn't know that was what her pupil was thinking, but she was thrilled with his progress. It wasn't long before Blueberry was walking around the school with Greg on board, crouched down low over his neck at first, so as not to startle him, then sitting up and talking to him, rubbing his mane as the little brown horse arched his neck in pride.

It was during these first lessons under saddle that Blueberry remembered Lulu's words about how difficult it was for horses to carry out movements with a rider on their back. As Blueberry stepped out in the school with Greg on board, he found he had to adjust his step and re-balance himself. Greg was a very good rider, making it easier for whichever horse he rode to balance beneath him. An inexperienced rider would wobble around, affecting their horse, but Blueberry only had to concentrate on himself because Greg sat so still. Nevertheless, it was still tricky for a while.

Whereas before (alone) he could walk, trot, canter and turn without thinking now (under a rider) Blueberry found he felt a little out of step doing all those things. He had to adjust his legs, his back, his neck – even his tail. It was a strange feeling, carrying a rider. No wonder Lulu had told him it would be difficult for him to perform all the lovely dressage movements in harmony with his rider. He was beginning to understand Carl's words when he taught his pupils, and the part both horse and rider played in making a beautiful picture. It was hard, this being ridden thing; much harder than the experienced horses made it look!

Orange wasn't quite such a star pupil; twitching and jumping when Sandra's other assistant Bryony first leaned across him, and spooking a little when she sat up. But it wasn't long before the two horses were walking and trotting around the school with riders, learning that instead of the trainers voice the pressure of their legs meant to move forward, and the closing of the rider's hands around the reins meant to slow down. These first lessons were very basic – the more subtle aids of the dressage rider would come later – and Blueberry learnt to turn left and right, to stop, to walk, to trot and to canter when his rider asked. And what a canter Blueberry had! Sandra reported to Carl that the little brown horse had a huge stride, and that both she and Greg found it difficult to keep up with him!

Sandra was also impressed by Blueberry's attitude. The little brown horse was, she told Carl, a model pupil; honest and willing – as well as brave. Whereas, out hacking in the countryside, Orange constantly looked out for monsters in the hedges and was easily spooked by a rustle in the grass, Blueberry, on the other hand, stepped out confidently, and only stared at something strange out of interest. This, Sandra acknowledged, was the sign of an intelligent horse. Blueberry didn't hear Sandra tell Carl this, so he had no idea how well he was doing – except when Sandra and Greg gave him lots of pats and praised him. The little brown horse was enjoying himself, and couldn't wait to go back to show Carl just how hard he had worked. He missed Carl, he missed Lydia and he missed Lulu, too. He had so much to ask and tell her. He wondered whether the little one-eyed dog was missing him, too.

Chapter Ten

"**Y**ou're back then?" said a gruff voice. Blueberry looked down and was overjoyed to see his old friend Lulu sitting outside his stable, looking up at him with her one eye. "I expect you've got lots to tell me – all about how clever you are now you're a riding horse."

"It was amazing," said Blueberry breathlessly, not quite knowing where to start. "I've been all around the farm with Greg and he said I was very good at being in the front when we were hacking – that's riding out along the lanes and in the countryside you know – and I wasn't nappy like Orange can be, what does nappy mean, Lulu? Oh, and I've had my first set of shoes fitted – listen (Blueberry scraped the floor of his stable with a front shoe, pleased with the metallic sound it made and noticing Lulu's nod of appreciation). I've learned to walk, trot, canter, turn, circle and stop and… hold on there's something else (Blueberry's chin wobbled with concentration) – that's it, I can also go backwards – that's ever so tricky with a rider aboard! It was all very exciting. When do you think I'll start doing passage and stuff?"

"Whoa, hold on there just a minute, kiddo!" exclaimed Lulu. "No use trying to run before you can walk. Carl will decide when you're ready for that sort of work – and it won't be for a long while yet. Remember those muscles we talked about? You don't want to strain them do you? You have to build up gradually to all the advanced work. Right now, you'll just be concentrating on the basics, and getting them spot on. There will be plenty of time to go passaging later. You'll have enough to think about, don't you worry."

"I suppose so," agreed Blueberry, reluctantly. "But I am glad to be back home, Lulu. I missed you."

"Don't go all mushy on me, kiddo," said Lulu, coughing suddenly and wandering off. But Blueberry could tell she was pleased to see him again, all the same. As Lulu wandered off, Willow, the big, fierce-looking dog, wandered by Blueberry's stable. Blueberry had never spoken with him before but welcomed the chance to do so now. Being a fully-fledged riding horse had given him confidence.

"You're Willow, aren't you?" he said. "I'm Blueberry."

"I know," said Willow. "Where were you found, then?"

Blueberry didn't understand the question. He just managed to stop his chin going into overdrive. "I was born in Holland," he told Willow. "Where were you born?"

"It doesn't matter," said Willow. "Nothing about *before* matters. What matters is where I am now. This is my home, here with Carl. He chose me – and that's the best thing ever, to be chosen. Did he choose you, too?"

Blueberry nodded. But the doubt that wouldn't go away, the fear that crept upon him in the still, darkness of the night, the problem that he had put to the back of his mind in his excitement at being a riding horse, returned with a whoosh. He decided to tuck away the dread that haunted him because of his lack of size. "Yes," he said firmly, "Carl chose me, too." And, as he said it, the fear subsided a little. His recent training had increased his confidence so much he felt that his plan, to be such a hard-working and willing horse that Carl would want him to stay and be his very own mount, was bound to work. He knew Sandra had been pleased with him and he couldn't wait to demonstrate his attitude and progress to Carl.

Hearing Carl's voice in the tack room, Willow bounded off. But Blueberry thought again about what the dog had said, and the way he had said it. What had he meant about *being found*? Blueberry decided he'd ask Lulu – she was bound to know.

The very next day Blueberry was thrilled to be saddled up and taken into the outdoor arena where Carl waited with the dogs. The family of guinea fowl bobbed along the side of the arena as though tied together with string, mirroring each other's every move and sharing anxious thoughts, holding panic at bay. Blueberry could see Willow watching them, his nose twitching, his gaze switching from the targets to Carl, and sighing when he saw Carl shake his head and warn him against pursuit. Lulu sat on one of the seats at the very end of the arena, curled up on a cushion, warm in the sun. Orange was in the arena, too, and Blueberry was led to the mounting block and mounted by Lucy, one of Carl's pupils.

"Hey there Blueberry," Lucy said. "I know

64

we're going to get on well!" Blueberry hoped so, too. He had hoped Carl would ride him, but realised it wasn't to be. Never mind, he thought. He could still put his plan into action, starting right now!

The horses and their riders, three in total, all worked in open order, in their own space. At riding schools most lessons are conducted in closed order, with everyone riding one behind the other, but, when training and riding at a higher level, each rider and horse finds their own space, so as not to be influenced by the others. This way each can concentrate on their own work. Blueberry was totally made up to be ridden in the huge arena with the mirrored sides at last. He had watched the other horses train here for over a year and now it was he, Blueberry, who was under Carl's tutorage, carrying Lucy, learning how to be a dressage horse. He put his excitement on hold and concentrated hard, his chin trembling.

At first it was strange being ridden around – especially when Blueberry caught sight of Lucy in the mirrors. It made him jump to start with but he soon got used to it. Orange took longer to get used to it. Twice he almost collided with his friend, Blueberry, as he darted away from the sides, startled by his reflected rider, and thinking he was about to jump onto him.

65

Everyone stayed calm and soon Orange was just taking a sideways step when he spotted the reflection, rather than diving half-way across the arena. There was a lot for a young horse to learn in his early lessons!

Blueberry hoped he was going perfectly – he could hear Carl suggesting how Lucy might help her mount in trot, and his advice certainly made the requests Lucy gave to the little brown horse easier for him to carry out. Lucy sat quietly and Blueberry found it easy to balance under her. Anxious to catch Carl's eye, he made his walk even more correct, his trot more rhythmic, and when Lucy asked him for canter, happily launched himself into the huge striding, powerful canter which had so impressed Sandra. Blueberry was delighted to see Carl's positive reaction to the strength and power behind his stride.

But as he cantered around, drawing admiring glances from Carl and the other riders, it suddenly felt to Blueberry as though his head was on fire. It was a horrible feeling, and not like anything he had ever felt before. So he shook his head, trying to shake the feeling out and away. He shook it and shook it and shook it again. Every shake of his head was more violent than the one before and, believing Lucy could be shaken right out of the saddle and onto the arena floor, Carl instructed her to halt!

Carl and Lucy examined Blueberry's bridle. Everything fitted perfectly – nothing was out of place. They took off his saddle and checked that there was nothing digging into the little brown horse – not on the saddle, on his saddle cloth or in his girth. They felt around his head, his neck, his ears – all seemed fine and Blueberry didn't give any indication of pain or discomfort at all as they checked. They were baffled. Blueberry was baffled – and upset. This wasn't part of his plan at all, and he didn't think it would help it. He hadn't felt like this when he had been with Sandra. He had never felt like this. And why did he only feel like this when he cantered?

Lucy mounted once more. Walking was fine. Trotting – no trouble, but when asked to canter the normally perfect equine pupil Blueberry turned into a head-shaking monster!

"It could be an allergy to pollen," suggested Carl. "We can try him in a nose net, they've been proven to help most pollen sufferers."

A nose net is fixed to the noseband of the bridle around the horse's nose, shielding the horse's nostrils from pollen. Some people are allergic to pollen, given off by plants during the summer, and in humans this is called hay fever. Many horses who suffer from pollen allergy find they can still work very happily with a nose net – but Blueberry wasn't one of them. If the cause of his head shaking was pollen, the net didn't have the desired effect. The violent head shaking in canter continued.

"Perhaps it's the sunlight, I've heard that affects some horses," said Carl. But when Lucy rode Blueberry in the huge indoor school adjacent to the arena after dark, with the artificial lights on instead of sunlight, Blueberry still shook his head like a demented dragon whenever Lucy asked for canter.

Guided by the vet, Carl tried herbal remedies; adding herbs and potions to Blueberry's feed. Many herbal recipes had good results with other horses – but not Blueberry. The herbs did nothing and the head shaking didn't go away. It was a real mystery – one Carl was anxious to solve. Here was a good horse, a horse he was sure had a brilliant future ahead of him. He had to find the cause of this worrying head shaking and help Blueberry.

"Gone a bit doolaly, have you?" asked Lulu, one evening, on her way past the little brown horse's stable. "Lost your marbles, head-wise?"

Blueberry didn't understand a lot of what the little dog was saying, but he got the gist. Unfortunately, he had no answer for her.

"I don't want to do it but I just can't help myself," he said, miserably. Since his head shaking trouble had begun, his plan to be the perfect dressage horse had been severely compromised – if not halted altogether. If he didn't get it under control he dreaded what Carl might do. A dressage horse that couldn't canter? Unheard of!

"What goes on, then?" asked Lulu. She felt sorry for her friend. He had tried so hard in all his lessons and she knew he was upset.

"It's like my head's about to explode," Blueberry explained. "I can't help myself. I think I might be going mad."

"Nonsense!" cried Lulu. "You'll come through this, kiddo. Carl is trying everything he can to find the cause – and the cure. If anyone can help you, it's him!"

"I hope you're right," said Blueberry, sighing. Then he thought of something else, something that he'd been unable to get out of his mind. "Lulu," he began, "what's Willow's story? He asked me where I'd been *found*, and said that Carl had *chosen* him. What did he mean by that?"

"Ahhh, did he?" said Lulu, sighing. "Well, Willow has had a hard start to his life. The horses here have been bred by people who know they will have a fine life ahead of them, working for their humans, competing and winning prizes – going on to glittering careers. A lot of dogs are not so lucky."

Blueberry listened intently. He hadn't

thought that the beginning of his life had been particularly special; he had known no other and the horses he'd grown up with all shared the same background.

"Lots of dogs find themselves thrown out by the people who should look after them. Maybe they have too many dogs, or maybe they just grow tired of them. Instead of finding them a nice home, some people – not very nice people – just throw their dogs away, especially if they are not pretty little dogs. Willow is part mastiff, an ancient war breed, and not everyone would think he was particularly attractive…"

"That's unkind," exclaimed Blueberry. He had always thought Willow looked fierce but he was still a very nice dog. Why were people so obsessed with how somebody looked – a dog who looked fierce, a horse which was small? It was very unfair, he thought, and took no account of a dog or horse's heart.

"Oh yes, you're right," continued Lulu, "and Willow has a heart of gold, something Carl recognised – and recognises in lots of dogs. Every dog deserves a chance, he says. So he likes to give them that chance."

"So where did he find Willow?" asked Blueberry, the words the mastiff-cross had said to him starting to make sense.

"At the dogs' home. There's a big dogs'

70

home in London and that was where somebody took Willow after they'd found him tied to some railings in a London park. Abandoned," Lulu added, in case Blueberry hadn't fully understood. "Thrown away."

Blueberry's chin wobbled. He felt so sad for Willow and for any other dogs who might have suffered the same fate. "So Carl went and chose him from the dogs' home?" he asked, the words Willow had said about before not mattering starting to make sense. Willow didn't want to remember the bad times, before he came to Brook Mill.

"That's right. Carl chooses the dogs he thinks nobody else will want. A big dog like Willow eats a lot, and wouldn't be at his best in a small house in the suburbs, if you know what I mean, which limits the number of people who might like to offer him a home. Here he has lots of space, people who love and appreciate him and a home for life. He's such a sweetie – but he looks like he'd eat you for breakfast. Oh – don't mention to him that I told you about his past. He's very sensitive about it and doesn't like to talk about it. Understandable, of course. He doesn't even know that I know."

"Okay," agreed Blueberry. "How do *you* know?"

"Oh there's not much goes on around here

71

that I don't know about," said Lulu, seriously. And Blueberry could well believe it. It wasn't until later, in the quiet of his stable in the dead of night, that Blueberry wondered whether his wise, short-legged friend had also found herself abandoned and unwanted. And whether she too, had been chosen by Carl.

Chapter Eleven

Carl sat on the seat at the end of the arena and watched the little brown horse named Blueberry working under Lucy. His hand drifted downwards to stroke Lulu and the dog snuggled up against his legs. Willow looked up, grunted and returned his head to his paws. He couldn't have Carl's attention all the time – he knew he had to share him with the other animals, too. Maybe, when Carl was riding, he'd keep a look out for those strange guinea fowl. Carl couldn't keep an eye on him all the time and Willow just knew the guinea fowl would be great fun to chase. He wondered whether they would still all run in a line, or whether he could make them go in all different directions. Oh how he would love to do that!

"What is making you shake your head, little Blueberry," Carl murmured to himself. The horse was fine in any pace apart from canter, which was the baffling part. Why canter? What did the horse do differently in canter that he didn't do in walk and trot? Carl refused to believe that this promising young horse had hit a problem which couldn't be solved. He knew there would be a reason for it, and he knew there had to be a way to overcome it – if he could only find out what it was. What key fitted this particular secret locked in little Blueberry? If he didn't discover the way to solve the head shaking, his breeding and his training would all turn to dust.

Dust…

Carl's mind raced and his heart beat faster as he made sense of his galloping thoughts. Canter is a pace of three-time, where one hind legs strikes off in one beat, the diagonal pair hit the ground together to make the second beat, followed by the last beat, the final foreleg. As

74

Blueberry cantered around the arena on the left rein, Carl could see his near fore, with its tiny white sock, lifting high at every stride. The horse had a powerful canter, it was his most extravagant pace, and the strength behind it created turmoil in the surface of the arena. In walk, the dust was hardly disturbed. In trot, Blueberry's hooves didn't make such an impact – but in canter…

"Lucy!" called Carl, hardly daring to hope that his thoughts could be right. Lucy turned Blueberry into the centre of the arena as her trainer ran towards her. "Take Blueberry out to the field, would you? Ride him around on the grass."

Baffled, Lucy did as she was told, heading the little brown horse through the gate and urging him into trot. Blueberry was confused. The field was where he enjoyed his turnout time with Orange. Why was Lucy riding him there?

"Try a canter!" ordered Carl, holding his breath. If he was right, and Blueberry cantered without shaking his head, the little horse still had a future ahead of him as a dressage horse. Lulu saw him cross his fingers behind his back, and she looked over to see what would happen when her friend changed pace.

"Wow!" breathed Lucy as Blueberry struck off into canter with just a token shake. The power was still there, she could feel the horse's hind legs gathering underneath her as he propelled himself along with his powerful stride – but his head shaking wasn't so violent. He still shook, but nothing like as much as he had in the arena.

"I think it's the dust!" shouted Carl, running across the grass. "Blueberry's huge stride kicks dust up into his nose. That's causing the head shaking!"

"But he is still doing it," said Lucy, "just not as bad as before."

The mystery hadn't been totally solved – yet! But Carl wasn't giving up. He knew that at each pace a horse uses different muscles, which means that a horse's head moves in a slightly different way depending on whether it was walking, trotting or cantering. There had to be another reason for the little brown horse's shaking problem. Carl decided to try out different bridles on Blueberry, knowing that different types and thicknesses of leather around the horse's head could make a big difference to its comfort, and even work on different powerful acupuncture points. After some experiments with all the bridles in the tack room (Lydia lost count of the number of bridles she adjusted to fit Blueberry's head), Carl finally found one which seemed to do the trick. The day the little brown horse cantered around the now dampened arena in

76

his new bridle, his head steady at last, was cause for celebration for the whole yard!

On that day Blueberry cantered with his heart singing. He would be a dressage horse after all! He could hear Lulu barking with excitement, sense the relief in his rider and couldn't wait to get back to Carl to receive the treat he knew would be waiting for him – a pony cube or sugar lump for being such a good boy.

With the reasons for the little horse's problem solved, it wasn't long before Blueberry's training was back on track and he continued his lessons. Everyone was thrilled with his progress – he had the most amazing attitude of any of the horses at Brook Mill. With his exuberant paces and love of his lessons (and his plan, which no-one but Blueberry knew about), the little horse was becoming a firm favourite with everyone at the yard.

Blueberry had begun his education in great style. Carl had overcome the problems with the head shaking and he was impressed by the horse's attitude and willingness to learn. But there was one thing still worrying Carl. It was the one thing no training, no great attitude, no bridle and no secret plan could do anything about.

Blueberry was still the smallest horse on the yard.

Chapter Twelve

Carl sat in his office and stared at the wall – not that the wall helped much. He was thinking hard, but however hard he thought, and however much he juggled things in his head, he kept coming back to the inevitable fact that the little brown horse in his stable who he had seen and liked so much in Holland, and had been so excited about buying, the horse which was a joy to train, was worryingly small.

Carl wasn't a short man – he was tall and leggy, and dressage riders ride with very long stirrup leathers so they can wrap their legs around their mounts, getting in close contact in order to give the light, invisible aids no-one else can see. The overall look of a dressage rider and their horse is one of grace, harmony and symmetry, and a horse which was well up to height, tall and graceful and able to carry Carl with ease and in proportion, was an important attribute. A horse, Carl thought, like Uthopia, the big black stallion, a year older than Blueberry. That was a horse which would carry him well. Carl looked out of his office window where he could survey the yard and see the horses grazing in the paddocks. There was Blueberry, next to his friend Orange. Even from that distance, Orange towered above the little brown horse.

"Maybe it's because Orange is so very chestnut and lighter than Blueberry," Carl wondered aloud. "Darker horses always seem smaller…" but he knew he was grasping at straws. He knew he was making excuses. Carl knew the little brown horse was too small for him. Why did it bother him so much? He had bought and sold horses before – some liked the dressage work and stayed. Others went well for other riders and Carl was happy to sell them on, knowing they would enjoy their lives in a different direction. Why did this little horse in particular matter so much to him? He'd only been at Brook Mill Stables a short time – but everyone liked him. He'd made an impact on everybody. Maybe it was because he'd been poorly, which had endeared everyone to him. Perhaps it was because Sandra had told them how willingly the little horse had embraced his early lessons, and how impressive he had been under saddle, even at this early stage of his training. And then, of course, Carl remembered how impressed he'd been when he'd first seen him in Holland – great paces, and a presence and intelligence which was so important to a dressage horse. They had to be quick and willing to learn – and there was no quicker or more willing learner than Blueberry. Carl sighed. He didn't want to lose him – but he just couldn't see how he would work out. Sometimes, Carl thought with a sigh, the right decisions were the hardest ones to make.

Carl had known that Blueberry was too small for him ever since he'd arrived but he'd held on to the hope that he might just grow and surprise them all. Horses don't always grow steadily – some grow in fits and starts; slow one year, fast the next. When Blueberry had stubbornly refused to grow any more than a modest sixteen hands high, Carl had reluctantly offered the

80

little brown horse to a good friend. He'd been delighted when she'd jumped at the chance to own and compete on such a horse, and Carl had been delighted to think he'd found Blueberry a good home.

But, just as the deal had been struck, something unforeseen had cropped up for the buyer and the home he had so carefully chosen for the horse had fallen through. Yes, it would have been the perfect home for the Blueberry, Carl had been certain of that, but now it was not to be.

Carl sighed again. The fate of the little horse had been on his mind for a long time – and even now he regretted the fact that however hard he wished, however much he thought about it, the one thing about Blueberry that needed changing couldn't be done, not by him, not by anyone. Carl simply couldn't magic a little brown horse into a big brown horse.

No one could.

Chapter Thirteen

"**C**ome along little Blueberry," gulped Lydia, putting his headcollar over his nose and fastening it. She sounded different, Blueberry noticed. Her voice was thick and she sniffed between her words. Pulling out a soggy tissue from her pocket, she dabbed at her eyes before putting her arm over the little horse's neck and laying her head against his cheek. This was a totally different Lydia to the one who had led him to the horsebox to go to Sandra's yard for his early training. That day, Lydia had been light-hearted and happy but today Lydia was upset, and Blueberry could sense her reluctance to lead him out of his stable and onto the yard where two of the other grooms came and patted him. They seemed sad, too. Blueberry felt anxious. Then he saw the horsebox, the ramp down, a deep bed of shavings on the floor, a haynet tied inside. With a start Blueberry realised it was ready for *him*. He was going on a journey. His chin wobbled. Where was he going now?

A dark fear gripped the little brown horse. Blueberry wanted to pull the rope out of Lydia's hand and canter back to comfort of his stable but he was too well-mannered. Instead, he allowed her to lead him up the ramp and tie the rope before kissing his nose, sobbing a goodbye and running down the ramp. Blueberry turned his head as far as his rope would allow and whinnied long and loud. Orange, hearing his friend's distress, whinnied back. But it made no difference. The ramp was lifted up and the horsebox rumbled into life, setting off down the drive.

Blueberry whinnied again, long and loud, his whole body trembling with the effort needed to make the noise carry as far as he could. He didn't know where he was going but he wanted to stay at Brook Mill Stables with Lydia, with Carl, with The Silver Dancer, with Lulu. Suddenly, he could hear his friend barking. Lulu, having heard the whinnying, was running as fast as her little legs would carry her, tearing after the horsebox as it rumbled toward the second gates.

"Blueberry!" Lulu barked. "Are you in there?"

"Help, Lulu!" replied Blueberry, even though he knew the little dog couldn't do anything to prevent the horsebox's progress in taking him away from his friends, carrying him away from his dream of being a dressage horse and of being trained by Carl.

"Wherever you go, always remember your dream!" barked Lulu, catching up with the horsebox as it slowed to a halt and waited for the second set of gates to open. Looking up, she put both her front paws on a wheel, speaking frantically to her friend. "Remember that you're in charge of your own destiny; you decide your future. Never give up on your dream, my friend, your dream to be a dressage horse. How much do you want it little Blueberry?" she barked. And then the gates opened fully, the horsebox changed gear, turned onto the road and carried Blueberry away from everything Blueberry wanted in his life, his desperate whinnying ignored.

He wasn't able to see his loyal friend, Lulu, running desperately after the horsebox until her little legs gave out. Her barks grew fainter and fainter as it picked up speed and carried the little brown horse out of her sight, out of her life. The little tan dog was left exhausted and panting by the side of the road, unable to believe Blueberry had gone forever.

"Welcome back little Valegro," said Mrs van Olst, warmly, calling him by his registered name – the one she had always used. Blueberry walked down the ramp of the horsebox and realised his long journey had brought him back once more to Holland, with his friends the van Olsts. He had wondered where he was headed – he had recognised the rolling of the ocean when the horsebox had driven on to the boat. He had smelt the salt of the sea in the air, just as he had when he'd crossed The English Channel with Orange. Only this time he'd been sailing *away* from Brook Mill Stables, and Carl, Lydia and Lulu, instead towards them.

The little brown horse didn't know if he would ever return to where his heart lay and he'd wondered where his journey would end. The uncertainty terrified him. Now, seeing Mrs van Olst, he was reassured in part at least. He had enjoyed his time at Mr and Mrs van Olst's, his second home after the farm where he had been born and had grown up with his dam, the lovely chestnut mare Maifleur. Everyone there had been kind to him. The van Olsts were skilled at teaching young horses to trust humans, to stand still for the farrier and the vet, to lead quietly and well, to behave politely in the stable, to stand square and to run up well in hand. He had learned good manners so that his further lessons as a ridden horse would be easy both for him and his new trainer. This second home had been where Carl had come to see him; where Carl had decided to buy him. Thinking of Carl made Blueberry sad. His dream had been to stay at Brook Mill and become a dressage horse – Carl's dressage horse. What was his future now?

Mrs van Olst patted his neck and Blueberry remembered, again, how kind she was and how happy he had been there. He found himself back in one of the big barns with the other horses. This was where he had grown up, with horses his own age, and recognising some of his old friends made him feel better.

Until they started asking questions.

"Tell us about your adventures," called Klaus, an upstanding brown three-year-old colt, with the tiniest white star between his eyes and a pink snip between his nostrils. "We heard

86

you had gone to the very top dressage stable in England, where riders learn to ride with reins of silk and the horses are all happy and live like kings."

"What was is like in England?" asked a grey gelding he didn't know. "Is it true it is always raining and everyone goes around humming *Land of Hope and Glory?*"

"What happened?" asked Mouse, a light bay mare. "Why are you back? Were you naughty? Did you misbehave?"

Blueberry gulped. There it was. The question he had been dreading: *Why are you back*? He almost wished he had been sent back because he *had* been naughty and misbehaved – at least then he would be able to make amends, to change his ways, but there was nothing he could do about the real reason. It was totally out of his control. He was back because he was too small. He had been rejected. He had been sent away, not good enough. No up to scratch. However he tried to word it, it always came back to that. It was no use trying to dress it up for the other horses. The fact was, he was too small to be a dressage horse – to be Carl's dressage horse. He was a *failure*.

Until he had found himself back at the van Olst's, Blueberry had clung to the belief that his dream could come true. While he was still with Carl he could be given a chance – he could show him how willing he was, how keen, how dedicated. But now it was never going to happen. A chance was all he had wanted, but he had been denied even that. He was no longer at Brook Mill Stables and he would never see Carl, Lydia, Orange or Lulu again. He was like Willow, he thought with a start – thrown away. He wasn't even Blueberry any more, no-one would ever call him that again. With the realisation that his dream was in tatters, the little brown horse took himself off to a corner of the barn, lowered his head and closed his eyes. He didn't see how he could ever be happy again, not now his heart felt like it was broken in two.

Chapter Fourteen

Blueberry's despair hung around him like a fog. Mrs van Olst turned him out in the field to graze the good grass and relax after his adventures in England, but the little horse held his disappointment in his heart and it showed. The spring in his step had disappeared and he carried his head low. Avoiding the other horses in the field he grazed alone in a corner, dreading them asking more questions, of having to talk about Brook Mill Stables and all his friends he had left behind. For days, Blueberry felt as though he was just going through the motions of living, without purpose and without joy, and he couldn't believe how heavy his heart felt – like he was carrying a tonne weight inside him, dragging him down into despair. He felt like a totally different horse.

Then, in his second week back in Holland, when the moon was bright in the night sky and Blueberry stood in the corner of the field, his head low and dozing, his mind drifted off into a dream. Blueberry's dream took him back to Brook Mill Stables and he could see Lulu and Willow playing in the yard. There was The Silver Dancer, lit up in changing colours, its foreleg lifted high in a dressage dance. The guinea fowl all bobbed along in a line along the hedge like anxious soldiers on parade, keeping a wary eye out for Willow, and Carl was there – smiling at Blueberry, telling him to *make it happen*. Blueberry felt happy.

But then the dream changed: Carl was frowning and shaking his head, telling Blueberry he was too small and the little horse, filled with dread, was once again in the horsebox, reliving the terrible time he left Brook Mill. Lulu was following, running down the drive behind the horsebox, barking – calling encouragement to him. He neighed back, calling for help, but his friend had been, and still was, in his dream; powerless to help him.

Blueberry twitched in his sleep remembering

90

the worst time in his life, straining to hear what his friend was saying. He felt it was important. The little dog had barked for as long as he could hear her – and probably longer still after the horsebox had sped out of sight – but Blueberry had been so upset he hadn't heard all she had said, or had perhaps forgotten. But now in his dream it was quiet and Lulu was still barking, over and over again, and suddenly Blueberry knew what it was she had said. He could hear it clearly.

Make it happen! Never give up on your dream. You can do it kiddo – find a way. Show them who you really are!

Blueberry woke with a start. He was still in Mrs van Olst's field but he didn't feel like the same horse that had gone to sleep by the hedge with a leaden heart and little hope. Carl and Lulu had given him the tools he needed to realise his dream. One dream would help him with another, he was certain of it. *Make it happen*, Lulu had said. And what else? *Find a way, show them who you really are!* Blueberry thought about his canine friend – she hadn't let the loss of one eye affect her life. And there was Willow, too. When he'd arrived back in Holland Blueberry had felt as though he had been thrown away, just like the big dog, but now he realised Carl had sent him back to the van Olst's so he was in the best possible place to find another great rider. He had tried to help him as much as he could.

Make it happen was Carl's mantra – and it could be Blueberry's, too. His life would take a different direction, but that didn't mean it had to be a bad one and his days at Brook Mill Stables would surely help him. He could still be the dancing horse of his dreams but just wishing it and moping about wasn't going to achieve anything, he realised. He had to *prove* he could do it – and the first person he had to prove it to was himself. He believed in himself, didn't he? Well now it was time to make other people believe in him, too.

Wide awake, the little horse stood in the corner of the Dutch field and remembered all the lessons he had heard Carl give, all the advice, the wise words, the philosophy he had listened to and absorbed. He thought of all the movements he had seen the older horses perform. He thought so hard his head started to ache and his chin almost wobbled itself right off his face. By the morning, Blueberry had come to a decision. He wouldn't let Lulu, or himself, down!

Chapter Fifteen

Mrs van Olst checked on the horses in the field several times a day. It was important to make sure they were all healthy and happy and that the fences were secure and the water trough was clean and full. Sometimes the grooms checked for her but Mrs van Olst liked the walk to the field, and she also enjoyed watching the horses as they grazed. It meant she had some time to collect her own thoughts and she found that she learned something about the horses' personalities and characters when she saw them together. Mrs van Olst was worried about Valegro. The little horse had seemed quiet and sad upon his return and she had already noticed that he grazed alone, rather than interacting with the other horses. She hoped he wasn't sick again.

Checking the water trough, Mrs van Olst was satisfied to see that it was full and clean and she wandered over to the horses to check them over. Yes, they were all upright, all grazing. No cuts, no-one was lame, everything seemed fine. But wait, she couldn't see Valegro. Was he alone again today she wondered, with a sinking heart. But then she spotted him over the other side of the field and yes, he was moving, he was okay.

Something made Mrs van Olst look again at the little horse. She looked harder. Then she put her hands on her hips and stared, not quite believing her own eyes. What was the little horse doing all by himself? No, thought Mrs van Olst, she must be mistaken. She walked closer and stood still again, staring at Valegro. Then she let out the breath she hadn't realised she'd been holding. It was true, she could see it clearly now, something she had never seen any horse do. Valegro, all by himself, and without the aid of a rider on his back, was circling in *passage*!

Mrs van Olst had seen horses in the field perform basic dressage movements before – all dressage is based on movements horses perform naturally – but usually she saw them when the horses were playing and interacting together. Stallions showing off to mares, excited colts with so much energy they thought they will burst if they didn't prance about but never, in all

94

her years breeding and dealing in horses, had Mrs van Olst seen a horse performing dressage movements without reason, all by himself, in a corner of a field. And Mrs van Olst noticed something else; Valegro's passage got higher and more elevated and more beautiful the more he did it. Valegro wasn't just performing passage, Valegro, it seemed to Mrs van Olst, was *practising* his passage. Valegro was *perfecting* it.

Goosebumps travelled all the way up Mrs van Olst's back and down again and she gave herself a bit of a mental shake. She must be mistaken. But no, the evidence was clear, it was there, she was looking at it. Only a fool, she thought, doubted what was plainly there in front of them.

Walking back to the house Mrs van Olst couldn't get the image of Valegro practising his passage out of her mind. The horse wasn't yet four years old, she remembered. He wasn't muscled up and fit, yet there he was, performing a very nice passage that wouldn't look out of place in a dressage test. Mrs van Olst thought hard. She would keep this to herself for now, she decided, and she would keep an eye on Valegro. Now she was in her own kitchen, making herself some breakfast, Mrs van Olst couldn't quite believe what she had seen. 'Maybe I imagined it,' she thought. 'I'll take another look later,' she decided. It was difficult to believe it when she was in her kitchen, surrounded by ordinary things because what she had seen – or thought she had seen – was so very *extra*ordinary! Mrs van Olst thought again about her doubts and not telling anyone else – she didn't want her husband to laugh at her or, even worse, think she was going mad!

So it wasn't until a few days later, because she had been particularly busy with a lot of visitors and paperwork that needed her careful attention, that Mrs van Olst thought again about the little brown horse. She thought about it because, when she went around the field one afternoon, there was Valegro cantering alongside the fence, changing legs. In canter, horses naturally change lead legs as they change direction. This afternoon, Valegro was cantering in a straight line and changing legs quite unnecessarily, every few strides.

Mrs van Olst stopped dead in her tracks and stood watching for a full minute before realising her mouth was open and if anyone had been watching her, they'd have thought she'd seen a ghost. Valegro's neck was arched, he flicked his toes and he looked to be concentrating very hard. So hard, he hadn't realised he had an audience. When he suddenly noticed Mrs van Olst, the little brown horse changed legs twice more, just to make sure (it seemed to Mrs van Olst) that she had noticed exactly how well he had executed them, before walking over to her and nuzzling her for treats.

"What are you up to my clever little Valegro?" asked Mrs van Olst, rubbing Valegro's ears. "I think you are trying to tell me something. And I think I know what it is…"

Mrs van Olst hurried back to the house, all doubts about imagining things firmly behind her. She knew exactly who she was going to call, and exactly what she was going to tell them. Mrs van Olst didn't think Valegro would be staying with them for very long.

Chapter Sixteen

Blueberry was too nervous to tug at the haynet in the horsebox. Where was he going now? Who would he meet? Was he finally going to a forever home this time, or was he on the way to a different life to that of a dancing horse? Could it be possible that he would never copy The Silver Dancer with his graceful piaffe; never to get to fulfil his dream? And who could say whether this next home would be his last? What if whoever had bought him now didn't like him, or thought he was too small, too?

Blueberry remembered Mrs van Olst rubbing

his ears as she led him into the horsebox, whispering that this was the start of an amazing journey for him – not just in the sense of another trip in the horsebox, but the start of his new life, his new career.

"I shall look out for news of you, little Valegro," Mrs van Olst had whispered, offering the sugar lump the little brown horse nuzzled for. "I know it won't be long before I hear how successful you have become. Go and amaze the world the way you have amazed me."

Blueberry's heart had lifted a little when he'd heard her. He wanted to believe that he could still make it as a dancing, dressage horse. He had to believe it! The trouble was, when the horsebox sped away from the van Olst's and Blueberry was alone with only his thoughts for company, they burst out like a firework in directions he didn't want them to take but was powerless to prevent. He had thoughts of new riders without Carl to guide them, riders with ideas about his future which didn't match his own, ambitions which lay elsewhere. And Blueberry knew he wouldn't be able to do anything about it, just as he'd been unable to do anything about leaving Brook Mill Stables and Carl.

The smell of the ocean reached his nostrils long before the horsebox trundled onto the ferry. The little brown horse wondered where he was heading for this time – England again? Wales? Scotland? Maybe he was destined for another country – one of the horses at Brook Mill Stables had come from Denmark and had told them all about how cold it was there. It seemed the horses spent most of the time in their stables, which had made Blueberry sad as he loved going out in the field. He hoped Denmark wasn't where his new life would begin. He was sure it was lovely, but he simply had to go out in the field – even if he would never again share his downtime with Orange.

The ferry crossing didn't take very long and soon the horsebox rumbled off the boat and sped on. The place smelt of England from what Blueberry could remember from his previous journeys. This time, he couldn't see out of the window and had only his ears and nostrils to inform him of the world outside. The haynet swayed to and fro with the motion of the vehicle, untouched by the little brown horse who was too anxious to eat.

The sun went down and Blueberry was shrouded in darkness, the street lights and headlights from other vehicles throwing shadows on the walls of the horsebox as it sped on through the evening. Blueberry wondered how much further he would travel and then, just as he believed they would be on the road

100

all night, the horsebox slowed and turned into a driveway. Blueberry lifted his head high and sniffed the air. He smelt horses, dogs, cats… all familiar smells. It smelt like Brook Mill – but he supposed all stables smelt the same.

'He's here!' shouted someone, and he heard cries and murmurs, hurried footsteps, dogs barking. They sounded like Lulu and Willow. Blueberry shook his head. Of course they did, because he wanted them to sound like his friends. That whinny even sounded like his old friend Orange. Perhaps he should have eaten the hay after all; his hunger was affecting him.

The ramp was lowered and bright lights from the yard flooded the interior of the horsebox, momentarily blinding the little horse blinking rapidly in the glare. Someone came to untie him, leading him to stand at the top of the ramp Blueberry peered out into the light, his eyes adjusting, straining to see his new home.

He had to be dreaming! There was Carl, Lulu and Willow, and all the stable staff standing in the yard, welcoming him back to Brook Mill Stables. How could that be? And then Blueberry realised the person leading him down the ramp was none other than Lydia, tears in her eyes, laughing as they stepped out onto the tarmac. Blueberry saw a chestnut head over a stable door, his friend Orange, whinnying his own welcome, and he just caught a glimpse of The Silver Dancer through the archway, changing colour in his own welcome.

"I knew you'd be back, kiddo!" barked Lulu, jumping up and down as though her little legs were on springs. "I heard Carl talking with Mrs van Olst on the phone – she insisted he was missing something special, and that you were one to watch. Carl was never happy about you going and Mrs van Olst certainly didn't have to say much to change his mind!"

Blueberry was so overwhelmed he could hardly think. Willow barked a gruff welcome and even his ferocious-looking face wore a smile. Blueberry couldn't tell whether he looked more like a happy dog who was fierce, or a fierce dog who was happy – but it didn't matter really. It was just as Willow said, *nothing about before mattered*. What mattered was that Carl was by his side, stroking the little brown horse's nose and looking very pleased to see him. Willow had been right about something else, thought Blueberry; it was the best thing in the world to be chosen, and Carl had chosen to give the little brown horse the chance to shine. Blueberry vowed not to let him down.

Lydia led him into his old stable and Blueberry saw that his bed was laid just how he liked it, his haynet was hanging in the corner and a small

102

feed waited for him in his manger. Taking a long drink he turned around and looked out over his half-door at the yard he loved so much, at the people and dogs he had missed so terribly. The little brown horse thought his heart would burst with joy.

"I knew you could make it happen, kiddo," said Lulu, her tail wagging at seeing her old friend back where he belonged. "Carl says you're here to stay, that you're headed for the big time. He says he'll find a rider for you as he's too tall to ride you himself. I knew you'd find a way to show everyone who you really are, just like I said. You're one smart horse and you deserve to succeed. I'm proud of you!"

"I couldn't have done it without you," replied Blueberry, lowering his muzzle to be nearer the little dog. "You gave me the inspiration when I needed it most – and you believed in me, too. You're a true friend, Lulu."

Lulu suddenly found something very interesting to look at in the corner of the yard. Blueberry wasn't sure, but he thought the little dog was holding back a tear or two. He understood how she didn't want anyone to see how overcome she was. She had her reputation as top dog on the yard to consider, after all.

That night the little brown horse, content at last, slept in his old stable next to his friend Orange, and with his good friend Lulu curled up under his manger, opening her one eye every now and then, just to make sure her friend really was back. He asked a lot of questions, this little brown horse, but Lulu knew he had it in him to be not only a good dressage horse, but one of the best. She'd seem horses come and she'd seen horses go, but there was something about this intelligent horse that Lulu had never seen before. She was relieved Carl had had the sense to bring him back, and was looking forward to watching Blueberry progress in his efforts to fulfil his dream.

Gazing through the archway, the little brown horse watched as The Silver Dancer changed from red to green to blue under the lights. A one-off, Lulu had called the statue. Well, he thought, he, Valegro, was a one-off, too. He would dance like that and do all he could to justify Carl and his friends' faith in him. His dreams were intact – he was going be the best dressage horse he could possibly be. He didn't know exactly the life which lay ahead of him but he vowed to try his heart out to make it a brilliant one. He wasn't going to waste his second chance.

The little brown horse, tired from his journey worries and excitement, at last closed his eyes and went to sleep, finally content. Blueberry was home – and he was home to stay. This was the start of his amazing adventures, he was certain of it!

If you enjoyed reading this book you may want to answer these questions or discuss them with your friends or class:

Chapter One

What do you imagine the horses in the yard were thinking as they stared at the chestnut and the brown horse walking out of the horse box?

Why does Lydia refer to Blueberry as *'a compact package'*?

Chapter Two

Blueberry thought the reflections were *'… strange, but it didn't worry him at all'*? What does this tell you about his character?

Why does Carl *'… feel the beginnings of a frown on his forehead'* ?

Chapter Three

Blueberry describes movement of the horse Carl is riding as *'dancing'*. What other words could be used?

Why does Blueberry think both Orange and Lulu might laugh at him?

Chapter Four

Why hadn't Blueberry eaten as much grass as Orange?

Lulu refers to Blueberry as *'my diminutive friend'*. Why?

Chapter Five

What do think *'cockerels announced the daybreak'* means?

What do we find out about Lulu's character in this chapter?

Chapter Six

Why would most horses be nervous of the Silver Dancer when they first meet him?

' "It's Latin," explained Lulu, without explaining at all. Blueberry made a decision not to go there.' What had just happened to make Blueberry decide this?

Chapter Seven

Lulu has the answers to all of Blueberry's questions. Why does she have so much knowledge do you think?

Do you think Blueberry is glad to be *'usually turned out with Orange'*? What are the pros and cons?

Chapter Eight

'It was the rider's job to entice the fabulous natural movements from the horses...' What do you think the word entice means?

What does *'riding is a partnership'* mean?

Chapter Nine

Why is Blueberry so excited to begin having a rider on his back? What does it signify for him?

Would you like Greg's job? Why?

Chapter Ten

What does Blueberry mean when he says that *'shaking his head'* wasn't part of his plan? What is he worried about?

What type of imagery is used to describe the head shaking?

Chapter Eleven

Why do you think Willow is so keen to have Carl's attention all the time?

The arena was dampened for Blueberry. What was the reason for this?

Chapter Twelve

What does this short chapter tell you about Carl?

What does it tell you about Blueberry?

Chapter Thirteen

Do you think it's better that Blueberry is unable to see Lulu running behind the horsebox? Why?

"We heard you had gone to the very top dressage stable in England, where riders learn to ride with reins of silk and the horses are all happy and live like kings." Why would be special about reins of silk?

Chapter Fourteen

What is meant by the simile *'Blueberry's despair hung around him like a fog'*?

What makes Blueberry remember Willow when he arrived in Holland?

Chapter Fifteen

Do you think Mrs van Olst's husband would have laughed at her if she'd told him what she had seen?

What is it that Mrs van Olst thinks Blueberry is trying to tell her?

Chapter Sixteen

'She had her reputation as top dog on the yard to consider, after all.' What does this tell us about Lulu?

Who do you think Blueberry was most pleased to be home with? What are your reasons for thinking this?

Blueberry extras

Blueberry beginnings

Valegro, stable name Blueberry, was born on the 5th July 2002 on a farm close to the sea in Zeeland near Rotterdam in The Netherlands. His breeders, Maartje and Joop Hanse, had put their lovely chestnut mare Maifleur (which means *May flower*) to the promising young dressage stallion Negro, owned by Gertjan and Anne van Olst. The resulting colt, named Vainqueur Fleur, impressed Gertjan and Anne enough to buy him when he was only a few days old – although they waited until he was weaned from his dam before taking him to their stables, of course. They decided the name Vainqueur Fleur (which means Winner/victorious flower in French) was too long, so they renamed the little colt Valegro.

As a late foal Valegro, was always smaller than the other colts but everyone thought he was well put together and was, from the start, impressive in his paces. I first saw him as a two-year-old, liked what I saw and decided to buy him – even though I thought he was quite an old-fashioned type. I always said he 'had the head of a duchess and a bottom of a cook'. This old saying harks back to the days when the gentry had domestic help. The duchess would supposedly posses a refined and aristocratic head, whereas the cook was traditionally more buxom, and likely to have the bottom of a person who likes to 'tidy up' the left-over pastries!

I buy several horses a year and not all of them work out for me. I always find them good homes and take an interest in their careers when they leave Brook Mill, but I cannot keep them all, however much I may like them. I liked Valegro's strength and his great attitude and I hoped he would grow big enough for me. Unfortunately, at four years old he was still only sixteen hands so I made the difficult decision to sell him. Although the person I offered him to leapt at the chance to own Blueberry, she was unable to go through with the sale and so I asked Anne and Gertjan if they could find him a great home. Valegro hadn't been back with them for very long before they rang me to tell me I should really keep him, they considered him that good. That's how I almost let the greatest dressage horse in the world slip through my fingers – but got him back in the nick of time!

What's in a name?

Naming the new horses is always a fun thing to do at Brook Mill and everyone likes to get involved and make suggestions. We like to have a theme every year – that way we can easily tell which year each horse arrived. In 2004, when Valegro arrived as a two-year-old, our theme was fruit and veg. Of course, each horse has his or her own registered name but these are often long and difficult to use on the yard and when ridden. Also, many of them may sound quite similar, and it's important for each horse to recognise its own name when we say it, because they certainly do. We called Valegro Blueberry because of his colour. It's a very unusual, chocolate colour which changes hue according to the seasons. And, of course, when he's clipped, it looks different again.

Blueberry was born black and his baby coat was a muddy brown, but once he'd shed his baby coat his signature rich almost black colour with a blue tinge shone through. This often happens with foals – you can get a surprise if you've only seen them at a few weeks old, and they turn up later a completely different colour! Blueberry has a lovely white star-stripe-snip combination, which runs straight down the very centre of his face. This is important – a wonky blaze can look as though the horse has a wonky face, which is not very good for a dressage horse! He also has four white legs – two smaller socks at the front and two much longer at the back, and this helps his overall look of symmetry, too. Have you heard the old rhyme that goes like this? *One white foot, buy a horse. Two white feet, try a horse. Three white feet, look well about him. Four white feet, do without him.* I think you'll agree, our Blueberry makes a total mockery of that old wives' tale!

Chill out time!

At Brook Mill, all the horses are turned out in the field for some time to themselves every day. I believe this downtime is vital for a horse's wellbeing. I don't hold with horses living in stables 24/7. I'd certainly hate being shut in the house all the time, and it would be detrimental to my work and temperament! It's important our horses go out to play with the others and form relationships and grass is, after all, the best food for a horse. Having balance in their lives encourages our horses to come to their work refreshed, ready and eager to learn and give of their best. Horses are our partners, not our slaves, and I hate to see horses unhappy in their work. If a horse is trained well and sympathetically, he will be your partner. This is a philosophy I encourage in all my pupils.

A head-shaking hiccup!

Blueberry suffered from headshaking when he was first ridden. This was a time of frustration for everyone concerned. Here was a fabulous little horse, with a tremendous stride and boundless talent, but as soon as we asked for canter …shake, shake, shake went his head.

I tried everything to help him – as you will have already read. The important thing to remember when something like this happens is that there will always be a reason for it – and finding the reason will give you the key to help. Blueberry didn't shake his head because he wanted to, it must have been even harder for him than for us as he was the one experiencing the discomfort. Eventually, I found the reason and the cure, but it was hard going for a while. When horses display behaviour like that they are always trying to tell us something. It's our job to listen so we can help them. I was thrilled to help Blueberry – and he has paid us all back in spades!

Expect the unexpected

We always have dogs around the yard. Dogs, cats, chickens, peacocks, doves, guinea fowl – we've even got a parakeet! It's important for the horses to get used to all sorts of sights and sounds. That way, they're not too surprised when they go to shows and competitions – although there is usually something there we haven't been able to replicate at home! Riders and horses need to learn to concentrate even when there are distractions. You may be able to perform a lovely dressage test at home, in silence, all alone – but when you get to a competition with an audience, music, flags, people running around and shouting, escaped balloons, barking dogs and whatever, it all goes wrong. If you compete, try to perform some dressage movements in different surroundings, to practise. You'll find it will really pay off!

Daily life at Brook Mill

All top stables have a routine and Brook Mill is no exception. We have the regular daily routine of feeding, watering, mucking out and grooming, riding and schooling, and then there are other regular diary dates for the farrier, physiotherapist, feed deliveries, lessons – it never stops! I have a great team of people who look after the day-to-day running of the yard which leaves me free to teach, ride and compete. However, there are plenty of other decisions which only I can make such as choosing what competitions everyone will enter, looking at horses which I might like to buy, paperwork and, of course, writing – not only the Blueberry stories, but various features in magazines and online. In addition, our Facebook page and website needs to be kept up-to-date – Blueberry has his fans and they like to know what's going on. It's a full-on life at the gallop, but I wouldn't change it for anything!

Don't miss...

... the next book in Blueberry's story! Now Blueberry is firmly established at Brook Mill his education continues. But who will ride him if he is too small for Carl? And how will his early attempts at competing in dressage competitions fare – will they be all he hopes for? Will the little brown horse be able to progress his dream to be a top dressage horse and emulate The Silver Dancer?

Glossary of equestrian terms

Action or Paces

The way a horse elevates its legs, knees, hocks, and feet

Bay (colour)

A reddish-brown colour of horse, with a black mane, tail, lower legs and muzzle

Blaze

A wide white stripe down the middle of a horse's face

Breeder

The breeder of a foal is the owner of its dam at the time of foaling. The person designated as the breeder may not have had anything to do with planning the mating of the mare or be located where foaling occurs

Bridle

Headgear used to control a horse, consisting of buckled leather straps, a metal 'bit' to go in the mouth, and reins

Brown (coat)

A very dark colour of horse, almost black, with the slightest hint of a lighter 'brown' around the muzzle, flanks and elbows

Bucking

A behaviour where the horse lowers its head and rapidly kicks its hind feet into the air

Canter

A smooth three-beat pace of a horse that is slower than a gallop but faster than a trot, in which the feet touch the ground in the three-beat sequence of left hind foot, right hind foot and left front foot together, right front foot. This applies to the opposite legs on the other rein (other direction)

Chestnut (coat)

A reddish-brown coat colour with matching or lighter-coloured mane and tail

Cob

A stocky, rather sturdily built small horse, that often looks like a large pony

Dam

The mother of a horse

Dressage

A classical form of horse training, involving the gradual training of the horse in stages. This training, if continued, can lead to an Olympic level sport based on classical principles of horsemanship, involving taking tests designed to gauge the training level of horses in classical dressage

Farrier

A professional hoof care specialist who trims

120

hooves and who also uses blacksmithing skills to shoe horses

Fetlock

The lower joint of a horse's leg above the hoof, where the tuft of hair grows

Gelding

Castrated male horse

Girth

A wide belt used to secure the saddle to the horse, which buckles to the girth straps on both sides of the saddle, running under the tummy just behind the legs

Grand Prix

In dressage, the highest level or test undertaken. It takes many years to train a horse to Grand Prix standard, and they must be at least eight years old before undertaking a Grand Prix test

Hand (measurement)

A measurement of the height of a horse. Originally taken from the size of a grown man's hand but now standardized to four inches. The measurement is taken from the ground to the withers. It is normally expressed in hands plus additional inches, so 15.3 hands ("fifteen-three") would be 15 times four inches, plus three inches – that is, 63 inches (160 cm). Abbreviated "hh" for "hands high" or simply "h". The European

121

system of measuring is said simply in centimetres

Headcollar

A device, generally either webbing or leather, placed on the head of a horse or pony for the primary purpose of leading or tying the horse or pony

Hock

The middle joint in the hind leg of a horse, that bends backward

Horsebox

A lorry specially adapted to transport one or more horses comfortably and safely

Horseshoe

A curved steel bar attached with special nails to the underside of the wall of the hoof, to prevent wear and provide grip

Leg-up

A way of getting on a horse's back, with a helper boosting the rider onto the horse with their hands under the (backward) bent knee of the rider

Lungeing

To work or train a horse in a circle at the end of a long rope or flat line (typically about 30 feet (9.1 m) in length), teaching it to obey voice commands and learn good ground manners, and to exercise it when not ridden

Long-reining

To work or train a horse with long reins from the horse to the trainer's hand used while the trainer is walking on the ground some distance behind or to the side of the horse. Teaches the horse to go forward on his own and can then progress to long-rein lungeing where the horse can walk, trot and canter in a large circle around the trainer maintaining an even contact from the trainer's hands to the bit in the horse's mouth

Mare

A mature female horse, usually four years of age or older

Markings

Generally refers to white markings on the horse's face, legs, and sometimes the occasional body spot on an otherwise solid-coloured horse

Paddock

A fenced enclosure where horses are kept

Passage

Dressage movement in which the horse trots in an extremely collected and animated manner

Piaffe

Dressage movement in which the horse performs a very collected trot on the spot

Poll guard

A pad designed to protect the horse's poll (top of head, directly behind ears) while travelling in a horsebox

Roller

Webbing strap with padding which passes around the horse's middle. Can be used to attach side-reins to when lungeing young horses

Saddle

A device placed on the back of a horse, where the rider sits, designed to support and stabilise a rider

Saddle cloth

A padded cloth, usually quilted, placed under a saddle to cushion and protect the horse's back, prevent rubbing and absorb sweat

Socks (markings)

A white marking on a horse leg that extends higher than the fetlock but not as high as the knee or hock

Tack

The term for all the equipment that horses wear such as saddles, bridles, headcollars, girths and other horse care equipment

Travelling boots

Padded leg guards that horses wear to protect their legs from any bumps or knocks while being transported in a horsebox

124

Trot

A diagonal, two-beat, pace between walk and canter

Walk

A four-beat pace, the slowest of the natural horse paces